Harmony

Harmony

A Treasury of Chinese Wisdom for Children and Parents

SARAH CONOVER *and* CHEN HUI

Illustrated by JI RUOXIAO

This Little Light of Mine   EASTERN WASHINGTON UNIVERSITY PRESS

Printed in Korea

14 13 12 11 10 09 08   5 4 3 2 1

Cover and interior design by Rich Hendel
Set in Arepo, Arno, SimHei and SimSun type by
Tseng Information Systems, Inc.

Library of Congress Cataloging-in-Publication Data
Conover, Sarah.
Harmony : a treasury of Chinese wisdom for children and parents /
Sarah Conover and Chen Hui ; illustrated by Ji Ruoxiao.
    p. cm. — (This little light of mine series)
Includes bibliographical references.
ISBN 978-1-59766-044-0 (pbk. : alk. paper)
1. Mythology, Chinese. I. Hui, Chen. II. Ruoxiao, Ji. III. Title.
BL1825.C66 2008
299.5'118—dc22   2008030758

EASTERN WASHINGTON UNIVERSITY PRESS
Spokane and Cheney, Washington

To the teachers, friends,

and friends-to-be who

cherish the cultures and

wisdom of the ancients,

and to all who find delight

in the many wonders of

China.

Contents

Above all else, prize harmony.

— Confucius

The depth of thought woven into Chinese culture is astounding. To acquire a thorough understanding of the historical mosaic that is Chinese wisdom — a mosaic composed of many millennia's worth of ideas expressed in literature, art, philosophy, religious traditions, and medicine — one would need to study innumerable texts. For this reason, we don't dare suppose that the twenty-four brief stories contained in this short book can do more than open a tiny window into the storehouse of Chinese wisdom.

Those two words alone — *Chinese* and *wisdom* — are worthy of a closer look. Who, or what, can reasonably claim to represent Chinese culture? Over the past three thousand years, many once independent ethnic groups have been assimilated into the mainstream culture of the Han Chinese, now the largest ethnic group on the globe. Today, over 92 percent of all those living in the People's Republic of China consider themselves Han, and yet Han Chinese culture is far from monolithic. From region to region, one finds variations in dialect, social customs, styles of dress, forms of cuisine, and so on. In addition, the Chinese government officially recognizes fifty-five minority groups. Despite making up less than a tenth of the Chinese population, these minorities are a significant cultural presence. The largest among them are the Zhuang, the Manchu, the Hui, the Miao, the Uyghur, the Yi, the Tujia, the Mongols, and the Tibetans. Although Han Chinese outnumber other ethnicities in most areas of the country, in parts of northwestern China, the Han Chinese find themselves in the minority. Some of these fifty-five groups have much in common with the Han Chinese, but others are culturally and linguistically distinct, both from one another and from the Han. In short, diversity is inherent in the term *Chinese*.

The second word, *wisdom*, also casts a wide net. If you ask a person on the street in Beijing, or in New York, what wisdom means and where it is found, you will receive a wide range of answers. Wisdom is insight into the world and its ways. Wisdom is the compass of morality. Wisdom is the knowledge that lies in our heart, not our head. Wisdom tells us how to refrain as far as possible from bringing harm to others, and to ourselves. Wisdom is the basis of religious doctrine and ceremonies. Wisdom can be conveyed in proverbs and stories. It can be expressed in music or in a work of art or glimpsed in the character of a person's face. The Chinese write the word *wisdom* (智) by combining the symbols for *knowledge* and *sun*, which could be interpreted to mean that, in the Chinese view, wisdom is the illumination that knowledge provides. No matter what the culture, though, wisdom seems generally to be regarded as the product of lessons learned from living. In turn, it must be applied *to* living, for wisdom both shapes character and is also its fruit.

The challenges we faced in compiling this anthology didn't end with the words *Chinese* and *wisdom*, however. Fundamental to much of Chinese thought is the concept of the *tao* (in pinyin transliteration, *dào*), a word that has no English equivalent. The Chinese character for *tao* (道) joins the symbols for *head* and *path*, suggesting a mental or emotional path, as opposed to a physical one. But the Tao is not a small path, one of many through the woods. Rather, it is something universal and fundamental to life—the Path or the Way with capital letters.

Viewed in practical terms, the Tao is the principle that governs appropriate action, the Way to right conduct. It guides us to behavior that will not result in conflict. But the Tao is above all a religious or spiritual concept. In this sense, the Tao is an all-encompassing natural force or energy that is immanent in all creatures and in the material world. Allowed to flow smoothly, without obstruction, this energy finds its own balance and so keeps all creation in a state of harmony. In nearly every Chinese formal garden, one finds a cherished limestone rock centerpiece, wildly sculpted by the elements of nature, a rock that looks more like water than stone. This is a concrete expression of the Tao — something that responds naturally to the forces of the world, that changes and yet endures. The Tao is not a synonym for God or "the gods" and is not usually worshiped directly. But this sense of the organic unity of all creation has infused Chinese religion and philosophy, along with literature, the visual arts, and medicine. Moreover, just as one needn't adhere to a particular faith to have a concept of God, one needn't be a Taoist to have an understanding of the Tao.

How best to capture the sense of these three key words — *Chinese, wisdom,* and *Tao* — was the puzzle we wrestled with as we began to assemble the materials for this book. We wished to avoid dividing the collection along religious or philosophical lines, with discrete sections on Taoism, Confucianism, Buddhism, legalism, and so on. After much thought, we eventually landed upon an approach based on set phrases known as *chengyu* (成語 *chéngyū*), a term most simply translated as "idiom." Anyone who is familiar with Chinese culture, whether on the mainland or in the Chinese diaspora, is aware that proverbs, maxims, folk similes, and other standard sayings are ubiquitous, not only in colloquial speech but in literature and the media. Some argue that Chinese culture is especially rich with this kind of communal wisdom because, for most of the country's history, roughly 90 percent of its people were peasants. Even today, approximately 80 percent of China continues to be agrarian, and one in ten people is functionally illiterate.

The chasm between oral, peasant culture and the culture of the literate classes has exerted a powerful influence over China's history. The Chinese written language, which was first codified during the Qin Dynasty (221–206 BCE), has long been an important element in Han identity. For over two thousand years, classical Chinese — its vocabulary and grammar — was the standard written form of the language, even though most of the population could not understand classical Chinese. The 1920s witnessed an energetic movement in favor of vernacular Chinese (*bái huà*), which is today the standard written form of the language, used by speakers of many different dialects.

Although *chengyu* were widely used in classical Chinese, and many *chengyu* can be traced to a specific written text, they formed part of oral tradition, and still do. They are one of the places where oral and written cultures overlap, which is one reason they appealed to us. The Chinese government has drawn on *chengyu* as a way to build a bridge between the age-old culture of the peasantry, with its reliance on oral tradition, and the emerging culture of a "new" China, better educated and more progressive. Today, *chengyu* continue to be common in both spoken and written Chinese, and they are a popular means to transmit collective wisdom.

By conservative estimate, the Chinese language contains about five thousand *chengyu*, although some dictionaries list over twenty thousand. Usually consisting of four characters, *chengyu* are fused expressions — that is, the four characters always appear together and in a fixed order. Sometimes a *chengyu* is essentially a proverb — a complete, short sentence that conveys a piece of wisdom. More often, however, *chengyu* are not easy to understand in isolation. Rather, they are very terse or compacted phrases that sum up a story (or the moral behind a story), and the story is therefore needed to explain the set phrase.

Most *chengyu* originated in early times, and many are associated with a particular historical figure or philosopher-sage. This is another reason we decided to work with *chengyu*. Because these sayings can often be traced back to a specific written document, such as a historical chronicle or philosophical work, we were able to present a fair sampling from all the major threads that have together woven the fabric of Chinese culture. But even if individual *chengyu* can be linked to a particular Chinese philosopher-sage or to a story preserved in an ancient text, the *chengyu* we have chosen for this book are very much part of contemporary Chinese culture. Each has stood the test of time, and each is familiar to the average Chinese person. It thus seems fair to say that these *chengyu* are representative of the culture as a whole.

Most of the *chengyu* in this anthology are very old, dating back almost two and a half millennia, to the closing centuries of the Eastern Zhou Dynasty. Prior to China's initial unification under the Qin Dynasty, the political landscape was fractured into numerous small kingdoms, and many *chengyu* contain none-too-subtle advice to rulers on how to gain and maintain power or how to achieve peace and political stability. In much the same way, the modern Chinese frequently use four-character idioms as shorthand to convey practical wisdom and ethical principles. In addition, the transmission of knowledge and community values through *chengyu* continues to play an important role in China's efforts to promote literacy and to mobilize the peasantry.

In his *Little Red Book* of sayings, Mao Zedong used the *chengyu* phrase *yú gōng yí shān*, which literally means "foolish old man moves mountain." The story behind the *chengyu*, which we have included in this collection, tells of an old man who digs away at a pair of mountains shovelful by shovelful, confident that his descendents will continue his work until the mountains have been removed. Mao used the *chengyu* to inspire the Chinese to make an unrelenting effort in the face of formidable obstacles. But it is not merely politicians who find *chengyu* useful. Young and old, rich and poor, parents and children — all those living in China know these sayings and the stories behind them, and they are mindful of the lessons they teach.

———————

Each of the twenty-four stories in this book is based on a particular *chengyu* and tells the story that goes with it. There are thousands of *chengyu*, making this a very small sample. Of the twenty-four we have selected, however, all but the last are quite common in everyday discourse. Twenty-four is also considered a lucky number in China. It is the double of twelve, the number of lunar months, and the Chinese regard doubles as a blessing. Chinese peasants divide the year into twenty-four solar seasons that mark plantings and harvests. A very famous Chinese historical work divides China into twenty-four dynastic periods, while the scholar Si Tu Kong divided traditional Chinese poetry into twenty-four styles.

Each chapter opens with the story as it appears in our written source. This version of the story, which is typically quite brief, is given in the original classical Chinese and in English translation. We then retell each story in a somewhat expanded form, in order to make the *chengyu* more memorable and vivid as well as to clarify its meaning. To lend a flavor of authentic Chinese storytelling and to encourage our readers to become familiar with the sound of the Mandarin language, we have occasionally included modern Chinese expressions, such as *tài hǎo le* ("Wonderful!"), in the retellings of the stories. These are always followed by their English equivalent, and a simple guide to pronunciation can be found in the back of the book. We encourage you to be adventuresome and try to pronounce the Chinese. As a friend of ours commented: "We Chinese have incorporated many English words into our language. One in every five people on earth is Chinese — so why shouldn't Chinese words become part of *your* vocabulary?"

China is one of the world's oldest continuous civilizations. To help orient the reader historically and culturally, we have provided a map and timeline at the back of the book, as well as short section that describes China's main philosophical and religious traditions. There is also a section titled "Source Notes." In this section, we identify the author or text from which the original version of the story was taken and make an effort to situate the *chengyu* in its philosophical and historical context. We also indicate how the idiom is used in present-day conversation.

It is our hope that these *chengyu* and the stories attached to them will enrich cross-cultural understanding and foster an awareness of how Chinese society has addressed some of the struggles we all face. We have tried to offer enough of China to pique your curiosity and stimulate a desire to learn more. Twenty-four stories may be no more than a drop of water from the sea of Chinese wisdom, but we hope they will give you a sense of the depth and breadth of that sea.

Welcome to a small offering of stories from China. China is one of the world's oldest civilizations, so this book represents only the tiniest bit of all that has been imagined and written in China over the past three thousand years. Because, today, one out of every five people on earth lives in China, it's important to know something about the Chinese and their culture. It's like making a new friend. When you first meet someone, you often spend time listening to stories your new friend has to tell—about her family, perhaps, or about the place she grew up or about things that have happened to her and made her laugh. In much the same way, to get to know Chinese culture you can begin by reading stories from China.

The main language in China is called Mandarin. It's quite different from English, partly because the meaning of a word depends on whether your voice goes up or down when you say the word. Also, the Chinese writing system doesn't use letters, the way we do, but instead uses symbols, called characters, that stand for entire words. If you'd like to learn a little Chinese, you can start with the word *tao*. It rhymes with "how," and the *t* is pronounced like a *d*, so the word sounds like "dow" (and it can also be spelled *dao*). In Chinese, *tao* is written like this: 道. The word *tao* is often translated as "the Way" or "the Path" because the Chinese character for *tao* combines the symbols for "head" and "path." But the Tao is a very special path. It is the great Way of nature, and it guides everything and everyone toward a state of harmony and balance.

Many Chinese believe that there is a natural energy or power that exists in everything on earth, not just in living creatures but in objects, too, such as rocks or trees. This energy is the Tao. When we behave in ways that interfere with the natural flow of the Tao, conflict and unhappiness are the result. So human beings should always try to attune their actions to the Tao. If we are selfish or greedy or stubborn, or if we try to force things to be exactly the way we want, we obstruct the energy of the Tao. But if instead we're gentle and patient and willing to be flexible, we allow the Tao to flow smoothly through us and around us.

Although Chinese culture differs from our own, we also have a lot in common. These days, a young person in China is just as likely as you are to be reading the Harry Potter books or watching TV or playing a video game with friends. But Chinese culture is much older than ours, and so everyday life is sometimes a mixture of old and new. For instance, the Chinese are very fond of traditional sayings or proverbs — short phrases that sum up a piece of wisdom or advice. These sayings are called *chengyu*. There's always a story behind them that explains their meaning and conveys a lesson or moral, much like one of Aesop's fables. Suppose somebody is being lazy. A Chinese person might laugh and say, "That's right — just wait by the tree stump for a hare." But unless you know the story that goes along with this *chengyu*, you won't understand what the expression means.

Each of the stories in this book is based on a *chengyu*. From small children to their elders, almost everyone in China knows the *chengyu* we've chosen for this book. When they're talking or writing something, the Chinese will often use one of these sayings to make a point or to poke fun at themselves or others who are being foolish. As you'll discover, sometimes the main character in a story is behaving thoughtlessly and so ends up tangled in a self-created mishap. Or perhaps trouble comes because the character is stuck in narrow mind-set and can't see the bigger picture. So a Chinese person might use a *chengyu* as a reminder or to warn someone about a possible mistake.

As you read this book, you may start to notice that, no matter what their culture, all human beings encounter much the same problems. Each time you read a story, see if you can find a similar situation in your own life—whether you were the foolish character or someone else was. Or maybe you know an adult who was doing the same thing as the main character in one of the stories. It's also good to think about what created the trouble. Did the person in the story somehow go against the Tao, the Way of nature? If you ask yourself questions about the stories, you may get new ideas about how to respond to challenges and solve problems—and then maybe you can teach adults a few things!

Most of the sayings in this book have been in use for over two thousand years, and the stories have been passed down from generation to generation. We hope that after spending some time with these stories, you'll be curious about Chinese culture and want to know more about it. You'll find some surprises in the stories, which is good—because when we come across something unfamiliar or puzzling and then try to make sense of it, we gain a deeper understanding of the world. That's how we become wise. Best of all, though, when you meet someone from China and you say you know the story about the farmer who pulled up all his sprouting plants so that they'd grow faster, you'll have something to laugh about right away, and you'll have made a new friend.

Harmony

杞人憂天 Qǐ Rén Yōu Tiān

杞國有人，憂天地崩墜，身亡所寄，廢寢
食者。又有憂彼之所憂者，因往曉之
曰：“天，積氣耳，亡處亡氣。若屈伸呼
吸，終日在天中行止，奈何憂崩墜乎？”
其人曰：“天果積氣，日月星宿不當墜
耶？”曉之者曰：“日月星宿亦積氣中之
有光耀者，隻使墜，亦不能有所中傷。”
其人曰：“奈地壞何？”曉者曰：“地積
塊耳，”充塞四虛，亡處亡塊。若躇步跐蹈，
終日在地上行止，奈何憂其壞？”其人舍然
大喜，曉之者亦舍然大喜。　《列子·天瑞》

A Man in Qi Worries That the Sky Will Fall

There was a man in the kingdom of Qi who so feared
that the sky would fall that he could neither eat nor
sleep.

Another man noticed him worrying and said,
"The sky is made of air. There is no place without air;
you walk through the air and breathe it in and out
all the time. Why do you worry that it will fall
down?"

The man of Qi responded, "If the sky is made only
of air, won't the sun, moon, and the stars fall down?"

The other man explained: "The sun, the moon,
and the stars are like a brightness in the air. No
harm will come from them."

The worried man then asked, "Will the land
collapse?"

Retelling

Cóng qián, long ago, in the kingdom of Qi, there lived a man so worried and so anxious that he rarely slept or ate. While most people look up at the night sky and marvel at the shimmering, winking stars, this man, having seen a falling star just once, lived in terror of stars plunging from the sky. He decided never to look up at the stars again.

While farmers around him rejoiced when thick, gray clouds ushered in spring rain, the worried man looked at those same clouds, pillowed high into great peaks and canyons, and fretted that they would surely come crashing down upon him.

As time went on, he worried more and more that the sky itself would simply collapse. People around him laughed at his panic: "The sky has been the sky forever. How can it tumble down?" But no one could explain to him exactly *why* the sky would not fall down, and so he continued to worry.

"The sky is simply air," said one old man. "There is no place without air on this earth. Think about it: ever since you were born, you've breathed it in and out without any problem! Every day you live with it and walk through it. The air is all around you. It leaves the morning dew on your doorstep at dawn and sweeps away the day's heat with an evening breeze."

The worried man looked even more distraught. "But what about the sun and the moon?" he said. "If the sky is just air, full of nothing, won't the sun, moon, and stars drop out of the sky and land on us?" The old man shook his head slowly, smiled pityingly at the worried man, and then looked up at the sky. "The sun, the moon, and the stars are like a brightness in the air. No harm will come from them," he said. "Why do you worry so?"

The man from Qi couldn't answer the old man's simple question. He himself did not know why he worried; he just did. Worry was his habit now, a part of him, like a shadow that followed him whether the sun shone or not.

So the worried man struggled not to think about the sun, the moon, the stars *or* the sky falling down. When the moon rose, huge and round behind the hills in the east, he turned away to keep from thinking about it dropping right out of the sky. When the sun reached its zenith — its highest point — in the daytime, he distracted himself with work, so as not to tremble with fear of the sun directly over his head. To keep from worrying, he made every effort to not look up.

One day, the worried man was forced to leave his village to conduct some business in a province far away. Wearing a peasant hat and traveling by foot, he avoided looking at the sky and stared only at the dirt road before him.

It had been a spring of heavy rain, and the road was muddy and in disrepair. On the first day, he came to a river that had overrun its streambed during the rains, carving away a large chunk of road. The worried man saw clearly, for the first time, that the forces of nature could move great swaths of earth. He exclaimed aloud, "Not only can the sky fall, but the land, too, can collapse!" Although distressed, he forced himself to calm down and continue on his journey.

On the second day, he noticed a number of rocks piled by the side of the road. Looking up to see how the rocks had landed there, he found himself at the bottom of a recent, large mudslide. "*Bù hǎo le!* It is bad!" said the farmer. "The earth falls down like the stars! The earth is collapsing! Nowhere in the whole world am I safe!" And the worried man turned around, ran home, and never ventured out again.

守株待兔 Shǒu Zhū Dài Tù

宋人有耕者。田中有株。兔走觸株，折頸而死。因釋其耒而守株，冀復得兔。兔不可復得，而身為宋國笑。《韓非子.五蠹》

Waiting for a Hare by a Tree Stump

There was a tree stump in the field of a farmer in the kingdom of Song. One day, a running hare hit the tree stump, broke its neck, and died. The farmer put his hoe aside to wait for more hares, hoping to capture another animal the same way. As the farmer never got another hare again, all the people laughed at him.

Retelling

Gǔ shí hòu, in ancient times, a certain farmer lived in the kingdom of Song. Working his land from dawn till dusk, as must all farmers, he toiled with little relief. The farmer had never anticipated an easy life, but one day, something remarkable happened that changed his expectations forever.

It was a hot day, noontime, so hot that the soil felt fiery. The farmer, tired, thirsty, and drained by the relentless heat, decided to walk to the edge of his field to rest under a large locust tree. He sat, despondent, on an old stump lying beside the tree. Year after year, generation after generation, his family had sowed this same field in springtime, tilled it all summer, and harvested it in autumn. In the best years, they had only food enough to feed themselves, with a little left over to barter at the market for supplies. When a crop failed, they fought off starvation, and sometimes they lost. He often wondered how he might improve his life and his children's fortune.

Refreshing himself in the shade of the tree, he closed his eyes and once again dreamed of a better future. Suddenly, he heard shouting. A hunter running through the nearby woods had flushed a flock of quail from the bushes. As the quail flew up in alarm, a frightened hare darted toward the farmer, as quick as an arrow, straight into the stump. When it hit the stump, it broke its neck and fell dead at the farmer's feet.

Delighted, the farmer picked up the rabbit and said aloud, *"Tài hǎo le!* Wonderful! How nice to get dinner without any effort! We will have a large stew of rabbit tonight!" The prospect of fresh meat, which his family had not had in weeks, made him hungry. He threw down his hoe and ran home with his prize.

Later, after the family had enjoyed their rabbit stew, the farmer lay down on his bed and thought about his unusual day. "I believe my luck has changed!" he said to his wife.

"Who can say there will be no rabbit again tomorrow? If I wait by the stump, we can have fresh meat every day." His wife smiled hopefully, for their life was not easy.

The next day, the farmer paid little attention to his crops. Instead, he waited on the tree stump beneath the locust tree, hoping that another hare might dash out and crash into the stump.

But the day passed and nothing happened. The hoe lay untouched on the ground. The farmer, empty-handed, walked slowly back home.

Two days, four days, six days passed, and still the farmer, waiting for another hare, did not budge from his post. His crops suffered from neglect. The village folk shook their heads at the farmer's folly: how could he depend on something so unusual happening again?

Three weeks later, the farmer still sat on his stump, unwilling to pick up his hoe. The weeds, now far taller than the farmer's crops, waved in the hot summer wind, as if they were laughing at him.

揠苗助長 Yà Miáo Zhù Zhǎng

宋人有憫其苗之不長而揠之者，芒芒然歸，

謂其人曰：「今人病矣，與助苗長矣！」

其子趨而往視之，苗則槁矣。《孟子．公孫丑上》

Pulling Up Sprouts to Help Them Grow

A man in the kingdom of Song felt pity for his slow-growing crops and so he pulled up their roots and replanted them on top of the soil. Returning home satisfied, he boasted to his family that he had helped his plants to grow tall. His son went to look: the crops had withered and died.

Retelling

Cóng qián zài sòng guó, long ago, in the kingdom of Song, there lived a hard-working but impatient farmer. Tending his wheat fields from sunrise to sunset, he labored through storms and blistering sun, hoping to provide food for his family. Yet though he watered each seed, weeded each row, and frightened the hungry birds away, he grew frustrated with the slow progress of his crops. "There must be something I'm not doing right," he fretted to himself, "some secret that will help them grow more quickly."

One sunny day, walking beside a row of tender seedlings to check on them, he discovered one that had fallen over into the irrigation ditch. He gently lifted up the sprout and replanted it on top of the row, covering the dangling roots with a few clods of dirt.

He stood up, put his hands on his hips, and surveyed the row. Much to his delight, the replanted sprout now stretched high above the other seedlings, to the exact height he had hoped they'd all be.

"*Hēi, yǒu le!*" he exclaimed. "I've got an idea! Why don't I pull up *all* the sprouts and replant them?" Hastening to the next plant, and then the next, and the next, he worked his way up and down each row, tearing the seedlings from their hold in the soil, placing them on top of the row, and mounding the dirt around them. He smiled and hummed as he worked, happy that his crops would be taller than those of his neighbors.

Finally, under the starlight, well past dinnertime, the farmer headed back to the village after replanting his last seedling. Exhausted but satisfied, he smiled broadly as he greeted his wife and children. He took off his *dǒu lì*—his farming hat—and announced, "I am a happy man. I have figured out the secret of making crops grow faster. We now have the tallest plants in all the kingdom." His family gazed at him proudly.

"Tomorrow," he said to his eldest son, "You must put your studies aside and come to the fields to see our good fortune."

"Of course, Father," replied the son. "I greatly look forward to it."

And without even eating dinner, the happy but tired farmer went straight to bed.

The sun had arced high in the sky by the time the exhausted farmer awoke the next day. The farmer's son, however, had dutifully walked to the field to see the result of his father's work. There, much to his horror, row after row of brown, withered seedlings lay crumpled in the heat, their roots dried out by the sun.

盲人摸象 Máng Rén Mō Xiàng

Blind Men Touch an Elephant

有僧問：'眾盲摸象，各說異端，忽遇明眼人又作幺生？ 《大般涅槃經》三二："其觸牙者即言象形如蘆菔根，其觸耳者言象如箕，其觸頭者言象如石，其觸鼻者言象如杵，其觸腳者言象如木臼，其觸脊者言象如床，其觸腹者言象如甕，其觸尾者言象如繩。"

《釋道原·景德傳燈錄·洪進禪師》

A group of blind men touched an elephant, and each came out with a different opinion of its qualities. The one who felt its tooth described it as resembling a long radish; the one who felt its ear said it was like a basket made of reeds; the one who touched the head thought it was just like a stone; the one who touched its nose insisted it was like a pestle; the one who felt its feet said it was quite similar to a wooden pillar; the one who touched its back described it as a bed; the one who touched its belly said it was like an earthen jar; and the one who touched its tail said it was like a rope.

Retelling

Gǔ shí hòu, in ancient times, in a small kingdom in India, there lived a ruler named King Mirror. This particular king was a follower of the Buddha, and he studied the sacred books and meditated every day. But in his kingdom at that time many other religions also drew followers. In the parks and markets, in the temples and schools, arguments erupted between defenders of different philosophies. Some people believed that they alone understood life's deepest secrets, while others held opinions that were exactly the opposite. Consequently, the king's subjects argued day and night.

The king worried that because people heard so many different ideas, their hearts would become confused. How would they know right from wrong? Wanting to lead his people back to Buddhism, King Mirror thought deeply about the problem. Eventually, an idea occurred to him that he hoped might forever end the bickering.

First, the king approached his chief councillor and asked him to gather, as soon as possible, all the men in the kingdom who had been blind from birth. The very next afternoon, the councillor came to the palace and reported, "Your Majesty, we have gathered all those who were born blind, and they are waiting for you."

Pleased, the king exclaimed, "*Hǎo!* Very good!" and thanked him. Knowing that these men had neither seen nor touched an elephant before, the king ordered that an elephant be led to the middle of the city square. He then called all his councillors, officials, servants, and citizens to gather in the square. They whispered excitedly while they waited, as they did not know what important pronouncement the king might make.

After a while, the blind men were led into the square. The crowd hushed when they saw them enter. "*Yí?* What's going on? Why are these blind men here?" people wondered. Soon after, the king's elephant lumbered past, led by its handler into the middle of the square.

King Mirror then addressed the blind men, "Have any of you ever seen an elephant?"

The men answered in unison, "Never!"

"Do you want to know what an elephant looks like?" asked the king.

"Yes!" they replied in one voice.

"But you cannot see it, so how will you learn what it is like?" asked the king.

"We will feel it!" one man replied.

"We will touch it," said another.

"We will hear it," said a third.

"*Hǎo!* OK, then!" said the king.

The great elephant stood calmly before them, and the king had the blind men form a circle around it. "Now," King Mirror commanded, "I want each of you to slowly reach forward and tell us what an elephant is like."

The first blind man happened to touch one of the elephant's teeth. "Your Majesty, I know!" he said. "An elephant feels just like the long, thin radishes I plant in my yard."

The second man, having placed his hands on the huge ear of the elephant, answered, "Ha! It is like a very large, soft basket woven of reeds!"

The third touched the head of the elephant and said, "Your Majesty, in my opinion the elephant feels exactly like a stone."

The fourth blind man touched the long nose of the elephant, shook his head, and shouted: "*Bú duì! Bú duì!* No! No! You are all wrong! The elephant is not like a radish! Nor is it like a basket or a stone. It's like a large pestle! Don't you think so, Your Majesty?"

The fifth blind man did not agree with any of the others. Crouching on the ground and hugging the leg of the elephant, he said, "Your Majesty, this animal is just like a wooden pillar. These men are not being truthful with you."

The sixth man, a tall fellow, could reach the elephant's back. Full of certainty, he said, "Your Majesty! The elephant is large and wide, just like a bed."

Meanwhile, a seventh man, feeling the belly of the elephant, said, "My king! I'm sure I am right! Isn't the elephant like an earthen jar?"

The other blind men shouted at him. "No, you're wrong!"

"A stone!"

"Like a radish!"

"A pillar!"

The eighth blind man, standing behind the great elephant and holding its tail, shouted, "None of you is correct! The elephant is like a rope! I have it here in my hands!"

And so it continued. The men could not agree with each other, nor could any one of them convince the others. Each insisted that he alone was right.

King Mirror looked about the crowd, at his councillors, citizens, and holy men, and saw that they had begun to laugh at the arguing men. The king, too, smiled. But soon he asked for their attention. "Those of you who don't follow the teachings of the Buddha also seem to be quite convinced that you alone grasp the nature of life," he told them, "and you want to argue on and on about it." King Mirror paused to let his words sink in. "Do you now understand that you are just as confused as these quarrelling blind men who know only a small part of the elephant yet are so certain of the whole?"

磨杵成針 Mó Chǔ Chéng Zhēn

磨針溪，在眉州象耳山下。世傳李太白讀書山中，未成，棄去。過小溪，逢老媼方磨鐵杵，問之，曰："欲作針。"太白感其意，還卒業。媼自言姓武。今溪旁有武氏岩。《祝穆·方輿勝覽·眉州·磨針溪》

Sharpening an Iron Bar into a Needle

The stream called Sharpen Bar ran under Xiang Er mountain in Mei. A boy named Li Bai once studied there, but he was not successful and quit. Passing by the stream, he met an old lady sharpening an iron bar and inquired what she was doing. "Making it into a needle!" came the answer. Li Bai was so moved that he went back to his schoolwork.

Retelling

Cóng qián, long ago, lived a boy named Li Bai. Although his father had very high expectations of him, Li Bai simply did not like school. His family sent him to a private school, but Li Bai thought that books were dense and difficult and hard to understand, so he didn't even try. He claimed that the books contained nothing interesting.

Li Bai often slipped out of the classroom without permission, finding much that fascinated him outside, in nature. One day, tired of reading and sitting still, he put down his book and slipped out to play. Taking in the blue sky and the warm sunshine, he wandered as far as the outskirts of town and found himself by the side of a stream. So he took off his shoes and waded in, hoping to catch a fish.

Li Bai walked slowly along the streambed, trying to snatch a fish whenever one brushed against his ankles. Before long, he came upon an old lady, sitting on the ground by the stream. She was sharpening a thick iron bar. She spun the bar, grinding it back and forth, back and forth, between a stone on the ground and one in her hands.

Li Bai watched her. Focused and determined, she worked extremely hard at her task. "Hello, Grandmother," Li Bai said, addressing her with the respect due an elder. "Can you please tell me what you are doing?"

The old woman looked up and smiled. Without stopping her work, she replied, "I'm sharpening this iron rod into a needle."

Confused because the rod looked far bigger than any needle Li Bai had ever seen, he asked, "You mean a needle you sew with?"

"Yes, someday it will be!" she said.

Astonished, Li Bai asked, "How can a bar so thick ever become a needle?"

The old lady looked up from her grinding. "That's an excellent question!" She smiled.

"You know that even a tiny drop of water, if it never lets up, will wear down the hardest stone. So how can I fail if I stay with it day after day?"

"But," said Li Bai, looking down shyly, "You are already so old. This job will take a hundred years!"

"Once I make up my mind to do something," the old woman said, "I see it through." She looked at Li Bai and smiled. "I will always be successful if I apply myself and don't give up."

Hearing what the old lady said and watching her earnest effort moved Li Bai greatly. In fact, it changed his life. From that point on, he understood that success depends on sincere effort and perseverance—perhaps especially in our studies, since they are the most difficult task we face. Anything, Li Bai decided, could be achieved if you worked at it every day.

So Li Bai returned to his school. He opened the books he had found so difficult and began to read. He worked hard each day, making slow but steady progress, and eventually he became one of the greatest poets and scholars of the Tang dynasty.

鷸蚌相爭 Yù Bàng Xiāng Zhēng

趙且伐燕，蘇代為燕謂惠王曰："今者
臣來，過易水，蚌方出曝，而鷸啄其肉，
蚌合而莫過甘喙。鷸曰："今日不雨，
明日不雨，即有死蚌！"蚌亦謂鷸曰：
"今日不出，明日不出，即有死鷸！"
兩者不肯相舍。漁者得而並擒之。今趙
且伐燕，燕趙久相支，以弊大眾。臣恐
強秦之為漁父也。故願王熟計之也。"
惠王曰："善！"乃止。 《劉向·戰國策》

The Fight Between a Snipe and an Oyster

The kingdom of Zhao was fighting with the kingdom of Yan, so a representative from the kingdom of Su went to mediate. He said to the king of Zhao, "While on my way here today, I crossed the river Yi and saw an oyster enjoying the sunshine outside. A snipe wanted to eat it, but the oyster closed its shell on the snipe's beak. The snipe threatened the oyster, 'No rain today, no rain tomorrow, soon there will be a dead oyster.'"

"The oyster replied, 'I will not open today, nor tomorrow, and there will be a dead snipe soon.' Neither would compromise. Then a fisherman came along and caught them both."

"Now Zhao is fighting with Yan, and their fight has already gone on for a long time. People are weary. I am afraid that the powerful kingdom of Qin will benefit like the fisherman did, so I have shared this story and my thinking with you."

The king of Zhao said, "Yes," and stopped the war.

Retelling

Cóng qián, long ago, the kingdom of Zhao fought fiercely with the kingdom of Yan. The fighting lasted for years, bringing much suffering and hardship to the people of both kingdoms. Because the conflict seemed to be at a stalemate, a representative from the kingdom of Su decided to mediate between the two. He asked to talk with the king of Zhao in hopes of persuading him to end the long war.

He was soon granted an audience with the king. After introducing himself to the king and describing the purpose of his visit, he asked to tell the king a story.

"By all means," said the king, "Please go ahead."

"Your Majesty," said the representative, "While I was on my way here today, I crossed the river Yi, and I happened to see an oyster warming itself in the sunshine on the shore, its bumpy, hard shell open just enough to let in the light. Not far from that spot on the shore, I saw a snipe wading through a marsh, poking its long bill into the mud here and there in search of insects, fish, or perhaps an oyster." The king smiled, certain he knew what would happen next.

The storyteller continued. "Naturally, after a time, the snipe spotted the oyster, and I watched as it approached carefully and noiselessly. But the oyster must have sensed the danger, because just as the snipe poked its bill into the open oyster for some soft meat, the oyster snapped shut. It caught the snipe's bill in its shell and held onto it as tightly as a pair of clamps."

The storyteller chuckled, as did the king. "Well, what do you think happened next? Who won the battle?" he asked the king. The king shook his head and said nothing. "I stayed for a long time," said the storyteller, "because I wanted to know the outcome. I watched as they stayed locked in battle — the snipe could not pull out any oyster meat, nor would the oyster let go of the snipe. The snipe could not even lift its bill, which was weighed down by the oyster. Neither gave way."

"I imagined," said the storyteller, "that their conversation went something like this. The snipe told the oyster, 'If you don't open your shell, you will begin to suffer from dehydration: no rain today, no rain tomorrow. Soon you will be a dead oyster!'

"And I imagined that the oyster replied: 'I will not let go today or tomorrow. You will never eat or drink again, and soon there will be a dead snipe!'"

By this time, the king's whole court was laughing at the story, thinking it merely entertainment. The representative let the laughter die down and then gazed at his audience in great seriousness. "Neither the snipe nor the oyster would give way. They could not agree to stop fighting so as to save both their lives. I watched as they struggled, concentrating only on their battle. As I looked on, an old fisherman happened to pass by. When he saw that neither creature could escape, he picked up the two in his net and took them home for his dinner."

"Now," the representative said, "the kingdom of Zhao has been fighting with the kingdom of Yan for many years. No one is winning. People are weary and have suffered much. I have told you this story because I am afraid that the powerful kingdom of Qin will benefit from your battle, just as the fisherman did, walking away as the victor."

A silence enveloped the court, and the king seemed lost in thought. "Your Majesty," said the representative. "Won't you call off this terrible war?"

The king of Zhao replied without hesitation, "Yes! Yes! I am finished with it." Then he sent a message to the king of Yan, proposing that they agree to a truce. And so the wise king of Zhao saved both his own kingdom and the kingdom of Yan.

邯鄲學步 Hán Dān Xué Bù

子獨不聞夫壽陵余子之學行於邯鄲與？未得
國能，又失其故行矣，直匍匐而歸耳。

《庄子·秋水》

Studying How to Walk in Handan

Have you heard of the young man from Shouling who studied how to walk in Handan? He couldn't get it right. He lost his original way of walking and had to crawl home.

Retelling

Cóng qián, long ago, more than two thousand years ago, there lived a young man in the Shouling area of the kingdom of Yan. Although this young man came from a wealthy family and was handsome and charming, he had little self-confidence.

Constantly comparing himself to others, he fretted night and day. Were his clothes as well tailored as others'? Did other families have more servants than his family? Did his family eat the best food? Did he make a good impression on everyone he met? The young man rarely enjoyed himself. Wherever he looked, he always found someone who had a more elaborate robe, or someone with a better-made sword, or someone who looked more handsome or was more learned.

His family members noticed his unhappiness and advised him to stop comparing himself to others. His neighbors also chided him, saying that he was too distracted, too concerned with others to dedicate himself to learning one thing well. But when people tried to advise him, this only fueled his feelings of inadequacy, and so he continued to suffer.

As the months went by, he began to doubt whether he even walked properly, for he felt, more and more, that he carried himself too clumsily for someone of his social rank. It was about this time that he chanced to pass by some people on the road who were chatting and laughing. Always looking for a way to better himself, he overheard one of them say that the people of Handan walked more gracefully than any other people in the world. Since walking was exactly what he was most concerned about just then, he decided he must journey to the city of Handan in the kingdom of Zhao and learn their elegant ways.

Arriving in Handan, he felt dazzled. Everything looked new and different, and he found that, indeed, people here walked in a way that seemed quite special. Watching some children play, he noticed that the way they ran from one thing to the next was lively and pleasing to the eye. When he studied old people, he liked their sure and steady gait. When he scrutinized the way young men his age swaggered, he was so impressed that he made up his mind to learn the Handan ways of walking.

Just then, a young man passed by. The young gentleman from Shouling thought it a perfect opportunity to learn. He followed closely behind, imitating the strut of this young man — swinging his left leg forward when the young man swung his, then swooping his right leg around and forward, just like the young man. But the gait felt unnatural to him. Before long, the young man from Shouling became so sweaty and tired from his concentrated effort that he had to take a break. The other young man, oblivious to his follower, continued walking and was soon far off in the distance.

Then an old man with white beard came strolling along, and the young man from Shouling followed him. But no matter how hard he tried, he could not walk exactly like the old man either. Eventually, the young man gave up. The old man walked away, and a young woman passed by. The young man from Shaoling did his best to imitate her, too, swaying ever so slightly with each step. Still, he never felt like he got it right.

Soon two months had passed, and all the young man's money had been spent on food and lodging. He had tried his best to imitate the ways of the people of Handan, but his lack of confidence had chipped away at any progress he made in a particular style. Little by little, in fact, the young man from Shaoling forgot how to walk naturally, the way he had his whole life.

Eventually, he was no longer able to walk at all and could only crawl back to his home.

埳井之蛙 Kǎn Jǐng Zhī Wā

埳井之蛙謂東海之鱉曰："吾樂與！出跳梁乎井干之上，入休乎缺甃之崖；赴水則接腋持頤，蹶泥則沒足滅跗。還（視）虷、蟹與科斗，莫吾能若也！且夫擅一壑之水，而跨跱埳井之樂，此亦至矣。夫子奚不時來入觀乎？"

東海之鱉左足未入，而右膝已縶矣。於是逡巡而卻，告之海曰："夫海，千裡之遠不足以舉其大，千仞之高不足以極其深。禹之時，十年九潦，而水弗為加益；湯之時，八年七旱，而崖不為加損。夫不為頃久推移，不以多少進退者，此亦東海之大樂也！"
於是埳井之蛙聞之，適適然驚，規規然自失也。《庄子·外篇·秋水》

A Frog in a Shallow Well

NOTE: *The ancient version of this story is somewhat longer than most of the other source stories in this collection. Rather than provide a full translation and then follow that with an even longer version, we have chosen to retell the story in a way that expands only slightly on the original.*

Retelling

Cóng qián, long ago, a frog lived in a shallow well, but he did not know how very small it was. One day, a friend of his, a turtle from the East Sea, came by. The frog looked at the blue circle of sky above him and noticed the turtle peering down into the well. The frog croaked, "Hello, friend! I am so happy you've come for a visit!" Hopping about in excitement, he added, "I bet you were just thinking how perfect my home is! I think it is, too!"

The frog jumped up onto the rim of the well. "See! When I want to go out, I can hop to the rim in one jump." Then the frog jumped back into the well. "When I come home, I simply hop down and find a cozy hole on the broken wall of the well."

The frog noticed that his friend the turtle did not seem impressed, so he continued to brag: "If I jump into the water, it comes right up to my armpits and holds up my cheeks so I can rest. And if I choose to walk in the mud, it covers up my feet so they never dry out."

The turtle still seemed unmoved by these facts, so the frog thought of a few more things to boast about: "When I look around at the wriggly worms, the little crabs and tadpoles, none of them compare with me. I am lord of all these waters, and so I am satisfied."

The frog thought it odd that the turtle had yet to offer some praise. Then it occurred to him that the turtle might not feel welcome in the frog's home. So the frog said, "My dear friend, why don't you come in and look around my place?"

The turtle smiled and slowly began to climb down into the frog's well. But before the turtle could get very far, his right knee got stuck in the well's small opening. The turtle hesitated, and then retreated.

Then the turtle explained to the frog about the great East Sea. "My friend," he said, "I live in a place so vast you cannot imagine it. Even the distance of a thousand *lĭ* cannot give you an inkling of the East Sea's width; even the height of a thousand *rèn* cannot give you an idea of the East Sea's depth."

The frog listened intently but was not convinced. He himself lived in the largest body of water he knew. But the turtle had more to say: "In the time of King Yu of the Xia dynasty, there were floods nine years out of ten, but the waters in the sea did not increase." The frog's eyes grew large at this fact. "And then," said the turtle, "in the time of King Tang of the Shang dynasty, there were droughts seven years out of eight, but the waters in the sea did not decrease." The frog looked confused and alarmed. "The sea does not change with the passage of time," said the turtle, "and it is so enormous that its level does not rise or fall according to the rain that falls."

"My friend," said the turtle, "I must tell you that the greatest happiness of all is to live in the immeasurable East Sea."

After listening to the turtle's words, the frog began to understand his own insignificance. Sitting in the dark, damp well, he looked up at the turtle and knew there were many, many things he had yet to learn and many things he had yet to see.

狐假虎威 Hú Jiǎ Hǔ Wēi

The Fox Borrows the Tiger's Power

荊宣王問群臣曰：“吾聞北方之畏昭奚恤也，果誠何如？”群臣莫對。江乙對曰：“虎求百獸而食之，得狐。狐曰：“子無敢食我也！天帝使我長百獸，今子食我，是逆天帝命也。子以我為不信，吾為子先行，子隨我后，觀百獸之見我而敢不走乎？”虎以為然，故遂與之行。獸見之皆走。虎不知獸畏己而走也，以為畏狐也。’虎以為然，故遂與之行。獸見之皆走。虎不知獸畏己而走也，以為畏狐也。今王之地方五千裡，帶甲百萬，而專屬之昭奚恤。故北方之畏奚恤也，其實畏王之甲兵也，猶百獸之畏虎也。”《劉向·戰國策·楚策一》

King Xuan, of the kingdom of Chu, asked his chancellors, "I am told that the people in the north are all afraid of Shao Xi Xu, the commander of my troops. Why?"

None of his chancellors could answer except Jiang Yi, who said: "A tiger caught a fox in a forest and was just about to eat it, when the fox said, 'You mustn't eat me. I was sent by Heaven to rule the animals. By eating me, you will violate the command of Heaven. If you don't believe me, just follow me to see whether the animals are afraid of me.' The tiger agreed and followed the fox as it walked around the forest. The animals all ran away upon seeing them. The tiger thought they were fearful of the fox, so he let the fox go free. He didn't realize that the other animals were really afraid of him, the tiger."

"Now, Your Majesty owns five thousand lǐ of land, with armed troops in the millions, and they are all under the control of Shao Xi Xu. The people in the north who are afraid of Shao are actually afraid of Your Majesty, just as in the story: the beasts were frightened by the tiger, not the fox."

Retelling

Zhàn guó shí qī, in the Warring States Period, when the kingdom of Chu was at its most prosperous, the king of Xuan was surprised to learn that people in the northern lands were terrified of his commander, General Shao Xi Xu. During a discussion with his chancellors, the king asked their opinion on this matter: why did the northern kingdoms so fear his commander? Only one responded, a man named Jiang Yi. He told the king this story.

Cóng qián, long ago, in a dense forest, there lived a fierce tiger who had a ferocious appetite. He devoured many animals each and every day, and all the small creatures trembled, fearing that they would become his next victim.

One day, the tiger was especially hungry but had found no prey all morning. Suddenly, his luck changed: he caught sight of a plump little fox strolling beneath the trees. Silently stalking the fox from tree to tree, he easily caught his prey with a single swoop of his paw. He opened his mouth to stuff the fox in.

In that instant, the cunning fox spoke up. "*Hèn!* Hey! Who dares to touch me?" he said indignantly. "What makes you believe that *you* are in charge of the forest? *Hèn!* Don't you know that I am the one sent by Heaven to take charge of all the animals? I was appointed the king! I rule all the creatures in this forest, including you! You will violate the command of Heaven and die a terrible death immediately if you harm a single hair on my head, let alone eat me!"

Confused and alarmed, the tiger stopped, holding the fox in midair. "How can that be?" he said to himself. "I am the king of all beasts, and all of them are afraid of me. How did this little fox receive Heaven's mandate to rule us all?" The tiger hesitated.

The fox stared straight into the tiger's eyes with stern confidence. Then he tapped the tiger's nose and rebuked him, "What's the matter with you? You don't believe me? Well, just walk behind me for a while! You will find that all the beasts scatter when they see me! Watch them—they run and hide, already half dead with fright."

Fearing to go against Heaven, the tiger thought it might just be a good idea to see whether the fox was right. He put the fox down and watched carefully.

The fox stepped in front of the tiger and swaggered away, pretending to make a show of his strength. The tiger followed closely behind. Soon they happened upon a flock of quail, which dispersed in an explosion of shrieks and feathers when they caught sight of the large tiger trailing the fox. The fox turned and smiled broadly at the tiger, acting as if the birds had run from him alone. "See?" said the fox. "See how they fear me!"

Next, they came upon a wild boar, distracted by the chore of digging for roots with his tusks. Startled by their presence when he happened to look up, the boar squealed and fled in terror at the sight of a large tiger standing right beside him. The fox turned to the tiger, gave a smug smile, and continued on.

Again and again, every creature ran for dear life upon seeing the fox and the tiger. With the fox directly in front of him, the tiger believed the fox's lie: by Heaven's command, the fox was the king of the forest. Thus the cunning fox won his freedom from the powerful tiger.

"And just so," said Jiang Yi, having finished the fable for the king, "Your Majesty owns five thousand *li* of land, protected by armed troops in the millions, and they are all under the control of your commander, General Shao Xi Xu. The people in the north who seem afraid of General Shao are actually afraid of Your Majesty, not the general, exactly like the creatures in the fable. You are the tiger, Your Majesty; the general is only the fox."

自相矛盾 Zì Xiāng Máo Dùn

His Spear Against His Shield

楚人有鬻楯與矛者，譽其盾之堅曰："吾楯之堅，物莫能陷也。"又譽其矛曰："吾矛之利，於物無不陷也。"或曰："以子之矛陷子之楯何如？"其人弗能應也。夫不可陷之楯與無不陷之矛，不可同世而立。

《韓非子·難一》

Once a man from Chu who sold shields and spears boasted about the firmness of his shield: "The strength of my shield can turn away anything in the world!" Then he boasted of his spear: "The sharpness of my spear can pierce anything in the world!"

Someone asked him, "How about piercing your shield with your spear?" The man from Chu could not answer. A shield that stops any spear and a spear that can pierce any shield cannot exist in the world at the same time.

Retelling

Gǔ shí hòu, in ancient times, spears and shields were the most valuable weapons of warfare. Soldiers needed both: the spear for attacking enemies and the shield for defending themselves. Naturally, warriors wanted the very best—unbreakable spears with deadly points, and impenetrable shields that were light enough to handle easily.

During this time when the finest spears and shields were highly prized, a salesman from the kingdom of Chu roamed city and countryside, boasting of his superb weapons. One day, he brought his shields and spears to a busy city market. Quite the showman, he stood on a platform and raised his shield above the crowd gathering around him. In a booming voice he exclaimed, "Soldiers and countrymen! Take a careful look at my shield! No firmer protection exists in the whole world." His audience murmured, impressed with the large shield glinting in the sun. He continued: "Like a magic charm, it defends the soldier against any enemy's spear, no matter how lethal."

Then the salesman put down his shield and picked up two of his spears. With one in each hand, he waved them high above the people's heads. "Come and look, come and buy!" he shouted with a fierce expression on his face. "My spears are the deadliest in the world! When your enemies know you possess one of my spears, they will run from the battlefield even before the battle begins! Nothing in the world is safe from its merciless blade. It can pierce the firmest shield. Nothing, not even stone, can stop it." He glowered at the crowd, hoping to impress them with the seriousness of his claims.

Mesmerized by his words, the crowd hushed. After a short pause, one young man began to laugh. Puzzled and angry, the salesman from Chu asked, "What are you laughing at? Am I not right?"

"According to your boast," said the young man, "your deadly spear can pierce the strongest shield in the world, while your shield, you say, is precisely that shield—the strongest in the world. What if you were to use your spear on your shield? What would the outcome be?"

The crowd began to titter and then to laugh heartily. The salesman could not answer. His face flushed red in shame, and he quickly gathered up all his spears and shields and fled.

鄭人置履 Zhèng Rén Zhì Lǚ

鄭人有欲買履者，先自度其足，而置之
其坐。

至之市，而忘操之。已得履，乃曰："吾忘
持度。"反歸取之。及反，市罷，遂不得履。
人曰："何不試之以足？" 曰："寧信度，
無自信也。"《韓非子.外儲說左上》

A Man from the Kingdom of Zheng Buys Shoes

A man from kingdom of Zheng wanted to buy a pair of shoes. He measured his feet at home, but when he went to the market, he forgot to bring the measurement. After choosing the new shoes, he realized, "I forgot to bring my measurement with me."

He went back home to get it. The market was closed when he returned. His wife asked, "Why did not you measure with your feet?"

He answered, "I would rather believe my measurement than myself."

Retelling

Cóng qián, long ago, there was a man from the kingdom of Zheng who wanted to buy a pair of shoes in the market. "But how will I know what size I wear?" He thought it over for a while, and then an idea came to him. He cut a piece a string, took off his shoes, sat on a chair, and measured his feet. He carefully cut the string with the scissors after measuring. "Ha! This is the precise size of my feet!" he declared. He looked at the piece of string with delight and put it down on the chair. Then he happily went off to the market.

At the market, he found the streets filled with people shopping. He stopped beside a small shop that sold shoes and started looking for pair. After a long time, he arrived at a decision: "These shoes are just right," he said, holding them in his hands and feeling the soft leather. "But I just don't know whether they are the right size for me!" he thought, and so he looked for his measurement. He searched in all his pockets, but it wasn't there. "Oh!" he suddenly realized, "I left it on the chair."

Feeling a little bit embarrassed, he said to the shoe vendor, "Sir, I'm sorry. I have left my measurement at home. Would you mind my going back and fetching it? I will pay for this pair of shoes as soon as I return." Before the shop owner could respond, the man had turned around and had started back home in a hurry.

Arriving home half an hour later, out of breath, the man from Zheng felt blessed when he saw that the string was still on the chair. "Many thanks to Heaven!" he said, smiling. "It is here!" He snatched the string and rushed back to the market.

The afternoon had grown late. The orange glow of sunset lit the last of the market vendors, who were folding up their stalls. The shoe shop was closed and shuttered. The man from Zheng trudged back home, disappointed, fingering the measuring string in his pocket.

His wife was surprised that he did not have the shoes. "Where are the shoes you needed? I thought you ran back to get them?" The man from Zheng, chagrined about his failure, told her what had happened.

His wife scolded him after hearing the reason. "How foolish you are! Why did you have to come back home to get the measurement? Why not try the shoes on with your feet?"

The man from Zheng said, "But I have more faith in my measurement than I do in my feet."

望梅止渴 Wàng Méi Zhǐ Kě

魏武行役, 失汲道，軍皆渴，乃令曰： '前有
大梅林，饒子，甘酸可以解渴。' 士卒聞之，
口皆出水，乘此得及前源。

《劉義慶·世說新語·假譎》

Quenching Thirst by Hoping for Plums

The army of the general of Wei took shortcuts, far
from roads. The soldiers all became thirsty and fell
into despair. Then the general told them, "There is a
forest of plums ahead, both sour and sweet, which
can quench your thirst."

The soldiers' mouths watered when they heard
this, and they marched on.

Retelling

Cóng qián, long ago, in the period of Three Kingdoms, Chancellor Cao Cao was not only a skillful politician but also a keen strategist, an able leader of troops in times of war.

One summer, Cao Cao led his troops against Zhang Xiu. The summer had been unusually hot that year. The sun burned like a fire, scorching forests and crops. The sky, cloudless, took no pity on Cao Cao's soldiers, who were trying to avoid the danger of ambush by traveling on arduous mountain paths instead of roads. But heated all day long by the sun, the hot rocks of the surrounding mountains seared them.

Well before noon, the soldiers' clothes were soaked through with sweat. They had neither eaten nor drunk any water all morning. Disheartened and weak, the soldiers lost their will to go on.

Then one of the soldiers said, "We will die if we continue without water."

The others agreed. A few men had even fainted from the heat. Cao Cao's march had slowed to a halt. Cao Cao saw that his soldiers would not, or could not, continue without water.

Cao Cao looked at his men sprawled along the path in misery. Not only would they lose their chance of winning a battle, but they might also lose their lives if they did not find water. But how could he inspire them and give them hope? What could be done right away to solve the problem of their thirst?

Cao Cao decided to send his two strongest men to look for water while the others rested. But when the men returned, they reported seeing no springs or pools, and all the streambeds were as dry as a desert.

Disappointed, Cao Cao spurred his horse and rode up a small hill that lay ahead of the column of soldiers. Just as his scouts had said, he could see no sign of a stream or a mountain pool. But farther off in the distance he did see something that gave him hope, and Cao Cao hit upon a solution he thought might work. It would be ineffective to order his troops to march if they had no hope. Pointing his horse whip in the direction he wanted his soldiers to move, Cao Cao shouted, "*Kuài!* Hurry up! There is water ahead!"

Hearing that, the soldiers looked up and asked, "Where is it? The scouts said no water could be found."

Cao Cao pointed and said, "From my vantage point on the horse I saw a large, cool forest of plums not too far ahead. Right now it is summer, when they ripen. The plums there will be big and delicious, sweet and sour," he said encouragingly. "Let's hurry along, and we will reach the forest of plums and have ourselves a feast."

When the solders heard this news, their mouths watered. Picturing the juicy plums, the soldiers felt almost as if they had the plums in hand. Their thirst subsided. Each and every one got up and resumed the march, eager to reach the forest that Cao Cao promised lay close by.

熟能生巧 Shú Néng Shēng Qiǎo

陳康肅公堯咨善射，當世無雙，公亦以此
自矜。嘗射於家圃，有賣油翁釋擔而立，
睨之，久而不去。見其發矢十中八九，
但微頷之。

康肅問曰：「汝亦知射乎？吾射不亦精乎？」

翁曰：「無他，但手熟爾。」

康肅忿然曰：「爾安敢輕吾射！」

翁曰：「以我酌油知之。」乃取一葫蘆置於
地，以錢覆其口，徐以杓酌油瀝之，自錢
孔入，而錢不濕。因曰：「我亦無他，惟手
熟爾。」康肅笑而遣之。

《歐陽修·歐陽文忠公文集·歸田錄》

Practice Makes Perfect

Chen Kang Su was so good at shooting arrows that
no one could compete with him, and this made him
proud. Once, while he was shooting in his yard, an
old man who sold oil put his load down and stopped
to watch. Kang Su hit the bull's-eye over and over
again. The old man nodded.

Kang Su asked, "Am I not good at shooting?"

The old man replied, "Nothing special—just a lot
of practice."

Kang Su said angrily, "How can you look down
upon my shooting?"

The old man said, "I know from pouring oil." The
old man placed a bottle gourd on the ground and
put a small coin that had a square hole in the middle
of it on the mouth of the gourd. He then poured the
oil straight down into the gourd, leaving no trace of
oil on the coin. The old man said, "I have done
nothing special, just a lot of practice."

Kang Su smiled and sent him away.

Retelling

Cóng qián, long ago, there lived a man named Chen Kang Su, a supreme archer. Praised as the best, Chen Kang Su knew no rivals, because no one was brave enough to challenge him.

One day, while he was practicing shooting arrows across a long field, an old man, a simple peasant who sold cooking oil, stopped on the nearby road and put down his load. The old man, who was carrying several heavy gourds full of oil, seemed to need the rest. He stood still, watching Chen Kang Su in attentive silence.

Sou! Sou! Sou! The arrows flew from Chen Kang Su's bow, forming a crowded cluster at the exact center of the target far on the other side of the field. Chen Kang Su grinned proudly at his accomplishment. Aware that the old man was watching, he glanced in his direction, hoping for some praise. But the old man offered only a small nod.

"Old man, do you know how to shoot?" Chen Kang Su asked. The old man said nothing. Chen Kang Su pressed on, "Well, am I not the best archer you've ever seen?"

The old man finally replied, "*Méi shén me,* it's nothing special, really—just a lot of practice."

Hearing this, Chen Kang Su grew angry. No one had ever responded like this before. "How can you look down upon my shooting?" he demanded. He shoved the bow toward the old man. "If you think it's so easy, why don't you take a try?"

The old man held his gaze. "It's true, what I say. Even though I can't shoot arrows, I know it from pouring oil every single day. Let me show you"

As Chen Kang Su looked on, the old man set an empty bottle gourd on level ground and placed a coin carefully in the narrow opening at the top of the gourd. In the middle of the coin was a small, square hole. Then he took a large spoonful of oil from another gourd, stood up, and positioned the spoon high above the coin. Tipping the spoon, he poured the oil straight down through the hole in the coin like a golden thread, never wavering once.

Skeptical, Chen Kang Su kneeled down to inspect the coin. Not a single droplet of oil glistened on it. It looked and felt completely dry.

Finally, Chen Kang Su stood up and faced the old man. The old man smiled: "I have no special skill. I've just had a lot of practice, like you."

After a pause, Chen Kang Su returned the smile, understanding the old man's gentle reprimand.

按圖索驥 Àn Tú Suǒ Jì

伯樂《相馬經》有"隆顙蚨日，蹄如累
麴"之語。其子執《馬經》以求馬，出見
大蟾蜍，謂其父曰："得一馬，略與相同，
但蹄不如累麴爾！"伯樂知其子之愚，但轉
怒為笑曰："此馬好跳，不堪御也。"

《楊慎·藝林伐山》

Looking for a Horse with the Aid of a Diagram

In The Art of Looking at Horses and Judging Their Worth, *Bo Le said that a fine horse always had a "high forehead and a high hoof." His son took his father's book to look for a fine horse and saw a toad outside. The son told his father, "I found a horse that fits your requirements, but the hoof is not so high."*

Bo Le knew his son was acting foolish, so he smiled instead of becoming angry, and replied, "This horse likes to jump; it cannot be ridden."

Retelling

Cóng qián, long ago, during the Spring and Autumn Period, in the small kingdom of Gao, there lived a bright, enterprising young man named Sun Yang. Even when he was little, Sun Yang dreamed of a great future and looked forward to the day when he could pursue it.

As soon as he came of age, he left his homeland and traveled westward to the kingdom of Qin. In those days, the kingdom of Qin greatly valued animal husbandry, especially the art of raising horses. The ruler of Qin had many fine horses, and he kept a large and skilled cavalry to defend the borders of his realm from enemies.

Because Sun Yang was ambitious, not long after he arrived in the kingdom, he became the chief official in charge of the king's horses. Sun Yang quickly excelled in his new job and was particularly talented at sizing up horses and judging their worth. Soon people dubbed him Bo Le, after a mythical figure fabled to be in charge of heavenly steeds. And so Sun Yang, now Bo Le, was often asked to travel through the kingdom to appraise and select horses.

One day, while Bo Le was passing by a farm, an old horse pulling a cart overloaded with salt neighed at him. Bo Le came closer. He saw that it was a truly fine horse, one that, if younger, could have covered hundreds of *lǐ* in a single day. The old horse was suffering under the heavy load, its flanks quivering from the strain. Its spirit now broken, the horse could once have galloped with the best across a battlefield. When Bo Le thought of this waste, he shed tears.

To help more people learn how to appraise horses, so that the finest steeds in the kingdom wouldn't be squandered, and to ensure that his unparalleled skill in judging horses wouldn't be lost when he died, Bo Le decided to write a book, which he called *The Art of Looking at Horses and Judging Their Worth.* The book brought him fame, and soon Bo Le became a general in the king's cavalry.

Eventually, General Bo Le had a young son who, although sometimes foolish, also loved animals. After thumbing through his father's book, the son thought that it wouldn't be very hard to find a good horse. He tucked the book under his arm and set out to find just the right animal.

According to his father's book, a fine horse had to have a "high forehead and a high hoof," and so Bo Le's son looked around for an animal that would meet his father's requirements. Before long, he spied a large toad among some tall grass. He opened the book again, making sure of the requirements. "Well? Does this animal not have a very high forehead?" he asked himself. He smiled, for indeed it did.

Picking up the toad, the son ran back to the house as quickly as he could. He burst through the doorway and shouted to his father, "Oh, Father, come see! I found a fine horse!"

General Bo Le looked at the toad in his son's palm and his face fell. "Oh? You would call that a fine horse?"

"Yes!" the boy replied. "I have found a horse with a high forehead that can cover hundreds of *li* in a day." He paused, a little disappointed: "Only its hooves are not very high." The general did not know whether to laugh or cry at his son's mindlessness.

Finally, General Bo Le replied, "This horse likes to jump; it cannot be ridden." He sighed and shook his head.

猴子撈月 Hóu Zi Lāo Yuè

佛告諸比丘：過去世時，有城名波羅奈，國名伽尸。於空閑處，有五百獼猴，游行林中，到一尼俱律樹，樹下有井，井中有月影現。

時，獼猴主見是月影，語諸伴言：月今日死落在井中，當共出之，莫令世間，長夜暗冥。

共作議言：雲何能出？

時，獼猴主言：我知出法，我捉樹枝，汝捉我尾，展轉相連，乃可出之。

時，諸獼猴即如主語，展轉相捉，小未至水，連獼猴重，樹弱枝折，一切獼猴墮井水中。

爾時，樹神便說偈言：

是等呆榛獸，痴眾共相隨。

坐自生苦惱，何能救世間。 《摩訶僧隻律·卷七》

Monkeys Dragging Up the Moon

The Buddha told this story. In the past, there was a town named Polona in the kingdom of Jiashi. There were five hundred monkeys wandering around in the trees. At a temple, they saw a moon in the water of a well. One of the monkeys told his partners, "The moon died in the well today; we'd better save it, or the long night will be dark." They discussed what they should do.

The chief monkey said, "I've got an idea. I will grasp the branch and you can take my tail. One by one we can make a chain and fish it out."

They did as he said. But before they could reach the water, the branch broke under the weight of the monkeys. All the monkeys dropped into the well. Then the god of the tree said, "You poor foolish beasts! All followed the one in front without thinking! How can you save this world?"

Retelling

Cóng qián, long ago, the Buddha told this story. In the kingdom of Jiashi, just outside a town named Polona, there was a temple. Thick forests surrounded the temple on all sides, and five hundred monkeys chattered to each other in the trees, filling the forest with commotion. Few people visited the temple.

One night, after the monks who took care of the temple went to bed, the monkeys jumped from the trees into the temple courtyard to play. Exploring, one came to the side of the well and began to investigate. He took a peek into the well, and to his surprise he saw the moon there, swaying in the water. Frightened, he shouted, "*Zāo le! Zāo le!* Oh no! Oh no! The moon died and fell into the well!"

Hearing this, the largest monkey came over and looked. "*Zāo le! Zāo le!*" he shouted, jumping up and down. The moon truly has fallen into the well!"

Right away, the eldest monkey ran over, took a look, and screeched, "*Shén me?* What? The moon has dropped from the sky and landed in the well! We must rescue it!"

In no time, the rest of the monkeys had gathered around the well and were climbing over each other to get a good look at the problem. A noisy discussion followed. "What can we do?" they asked one another. "We have to save the moon!"

The old monkey quieted the crowd. "We should work together as a group," he said, "to get the moon out right away. The whole world will be forever dark, every night, if the moon sinks in the well."

But how could they fish the moon from a well, they wondered. The old monkey saw that just beside them a tree leaned over the well. He slapped his hand to his head, "*Wǒ yǒu le!* I have an idea! Do exactly what I say and we can fish the moon out for sure."

He brought over a bottle gourd and gave it to the smallest monkey. "Use this water gourd to scoop up the moon," he told him. To the crowd he said, "Follow my instructions."

The old monkey stood by the tree and asked the strongest to climb it. When the monkey was high in the tree, he told the others, "Now another of you climb the tree and hold on to his tail. This way, one by one, holding each other's tails, we can drop into the well and save the moon." The large monkey hung onto the tree, and hand to tail, one after another, the other monkeys formed a long line, like a chain. The smallest monkey, still holding the water gourd, reached the water first.

He stretched out his arm and tried to use the gourd to scoop up the moon, but he could not catch it. The moon broke into a hundred pieces as soon as he touched the water. When he looked into his gourd, though, he saw the round moon, a little smaller, floating on the water. It seemed that the moon was playing hide and seek with him.

But just as the small monkey noticed this, the tree branch cracked and broke off. All the monkeys who had helped fell into the water and drowned. The others scattered in dismay.

Saddened by this sight, the god of the tree spoke to them. "You poor, foolish beasts! Every monkey followed the one in front without thinking! How can you save the world?" And the Buddha concluded by saying that, however much they want to help others, when people aren't wise, they cannot even save themselves.

亡羊補牢 Wáng Yáng Bǔ Láo

Mend the Sheepfold, Even If Sheep Have Been Lost

庄辛謂楚襄王曰：“君王左州侯，右夏侯，輦從鄢陵君與壽陵君，專淫逸侈靡，不顧國政，郢都必危矣。”襄王曰：“先生老悖乎？將以為楚國妖祥乎？”庄辛曰：“臣誠見其必然者也。非敢以為國妖祥也。君王卒幸四子者不衰，楚國必亡矣。臣請辟於趙，淹留以觀之。”

庄辛去之趙，留五月，秦果舉鄢、郢、巫、上蔡、陳之地，襄王流揜於城陽。於是使人發騶，征庄辛於趙。庄辛曰：“諾。”

庄辛至，襄王曰：“寡人不能用先生之言，今事至於此，為之奈何？”

庄辛對曰：“臣聞鄙語曰：‘見兔而顧犬，未為晚也；亡羊而補牢，未為遲也。’臣聞昔湯、武以百裡昌，桀、紂以天下亡。今楚國雖小，絕長續短，猶以數千裡，豈特百裡哉？ 《劉向·戰國策．楚策》

Zhuan Xin, a minister of the kingdom of Chu, said, "I heard a saying: 'It is never too late to send your hunting dog out for your prey, nor is it ever too late to mend the fold, even after some sheep have been lost.' King Tang of Shang and King Wu of Zhou had prosperous kingdoms, even though they had only a few hundred acres of land, while King Jie of Xia and King Zhou of Ying lost their kingdoms and were killed, even though they had vast lands. Although the kingdom of Chu is small, it has the potential to grow vast and strong because its rulers build upon their advantages and learn from their mistakes."

Retelling

Gǔ shí hòu, in ancient times, during the great conflicts between kingdoms, there existed a small kingdom called Chu. Now, the king of Chu, along with his trusted court officials, frittered away their time and treasury in entertainment and luxuries. Indulging in feasts, jewels, and silks, they did not look outside the palace walls: they did not see that the more they enjoyed themselves, the more the kingdom and its poor suffered.

But a single honest minister, Zhuan Xin, stood outside the daily revels and entertainment, keeping watch over the kingdom's affairs. He alone foresaw that the kingdom's future was in peril because of royal excesses. Finally, he could no longer keep the size of the problems a secret. He knew he must tell the king.

"Your Majesty," said Zhuan Xin, "Your kingdom is on the verge of collapse and you don't know it. You've surrounded yourself with flatterers who tell you what you want to hear. Your treasury is nearly empty, the food reserves across the land have shrunk to nothing, and enemies infiltrate your unprotected borders."

Affronted by this startling news, the king looked at Zhuan Xin suspiciously. "How dare you spread a rumor like this throughout the country! You are putting a curse upon us!"

Zhuan Xin bowed deeply, humbly. "I have not said a word to anyone, Your Majesty. But the peasants outside this palace already know of our dire situation. They live in fear of starvation and in fear of our enemies."

"I think you worry far, far too much," said the king. "None of my other ministers has mentioned even a word of this."

"Sire," said Zhuan Xin, "If you go on like this, the kingdom will perish, sooner or later. I beg you to heed my advice."

The king did not respond. Zhuan Xin knew that the king did not believe him. "Please," said Zhuan Xin, "if you don't trust my council, let me travel to another kingdom and find work as an advisor there."

"As you wish," said the king, turning to his other ministers, laughing off the gloomy predictions.

Zhuan Xin soon took his leave and traveled to the state of Zhao.

Five months later, the king of Qin invaded the kingdom of Chu, just as Zhuan Xin had forecast. With much of his territory under siege, the king of Chu took refuge temporarily in another land to develop a strategy for recapturing his kingdom. But, amid the chaos, the king remembered his prophetic minister, Zhuan Xin, and sent his men to fetch him.

A week later, Zhuan Xin appeared before the exiled king and his court, sad to see the king in such unfortunate circumstances.

The king, anxious for advice, asked him, "What can I do now? Is there any hope for my kingdom?"

Zhuan Xin, looking thoughtful, replied with a story: "Once, a long time ago, a shepherd led his sheep daily into the thick, green meadows of the mountains. At night, he brought them back to his sheepfold, which he had carefully constructed out of sticks and branches, down in a ravine. Awake and vigilant all night long, the shepherd kept the sheep safe from wolves and other predators. This was his routine year after year: fattening the lambs for market during the day and protecting them at night. And so he prospered."

Zhuan Xin continued. "At some point, perhaps because he was so accustomed to his success, the herder became a little lazy, or perhaps a little reckless. He rarely searched for holes in his fence, and he slept through the night as if under a pile of quilts in his village home. But one day when he awoke, a lamb was missing. Although angry and upset, the herder felt confident that it wouldn't happen again. After all, nothing like this had ever happened before."

Zhuan Xin caught the king's gaze. "The herder was wrong," he said.

"Another lamb disappeared, and then another. Irate, the herder fumed to the village folk about the wolves, but no one else had lost any sheep.

"Finally, one villager asked him, 'Have you taken good care of the fold? Have you examined each branch and twig for any sign of weakness?' The herder admitted that he hadn't.

"'Then you must do that right away,' said the villager. 'You must search for your mistakes and correct them. If you do not repeat mistakes, you will soon prosper again.'"

Zhuan Xin surveyed the king and his councillors, all of them in grave distress, much like the shepherd. "Sire," he said, "it is not too late for you to mend the sheepfold, even though some of the sheep are missing. It's never too late to learn from mistakes."

The king nodded slowly. He understood why Zhuan Xin had told his court the story. Saving his kingdom would require a mighty effort, but it wasn't too late to mend his ways. He hadn't lost everything.

Zhuan Xin, now respected by all at court, offered the king many practical suggestions for replenishing the kingdom's wealth and securing its borders. The king was very much pleased, and from that time onward he listened closely to his most trusted advisor, Zhuan Xin. Because the king learned to reflect upon each mistake in order not to repeat it, the kingdom of Chu once again grew stable and prosperous.

南轅北轍 Nán Yuán Běi Zhé

Trying to Go South by Driving the Chariot North

魏王欲攻邯鄲，季梁聞之，中道而反；衣焦不申，頭塵不去，往見王曰："今者臣來，見人於大行。方北面而持其駕，告臣曰：'我欲之楚。'臣曰：'君之楚，將奚為北面?'曰：'吾馬良！'臣曰：'馬雖良，此非楚之路也。'曰：'吾用多！'臣曰：'用雖多，此非楚之路也。'曰：'吾御者善！'此數者愈善，而離楚愈遠矣。"今王動欲成霸王，舉欲信於天下。恃王國之大，兵之精銳，而攻邯鄲，以廣地尊名。王之動愈數，而離王愈遠耳。猶至楚而北行也。"《劉向·戰國策·魏策四》

The rich and powerful king of Wei wanted to attack the capital of the smaller and weaker kingdom of Zhao. An official of the kingdom of Wei, Ji Liang, heard news of the impending attack after he had left on a diplomatic trip. Even though he was halfway to his destination, he turned right around. Unwashed and in wrinkled clothes, he hurried into the palace to see the king.

Ji Liang said to the king: "On my way here today, I met somebody on the road. He was going north and told me, 'I want to go to kingdom of Chu.'

"I said to him, 'The kingdom of Chu is to the south of Wei. How you can get there by going north?'

"He replied, 'My horses are good.'

"I was confused. 'Even though your horses are good, this is not the road to Chu,' I said.

"He replied, 'I have a lot of money to pay for my trip.'

"I said to him, 'Though you may have more than enough money, this is not the road to Chu!'

"He told me, 'Yes, but my driver is very skilled.' Yet no matter how many advantages he had, he traveled farther and farther from Chu.

"Now," said Ji Liang, "Your Majesty wants to control the whole world and to gain the world's trust by your every action. Your Majesty has vast lands and a very good army. However, attacking Zhao, a poor and small country, is similar to the man who wants to go south by driving north. The more wrong action you take, the farther away you will be from your purpose."

Retelling

Gǔ shí hòu, in ancient times, during the Warring States Period, the kingdom of Wei wanted to control all the other kingdoms. And so the king of Wei planned to attack small, poor Handan, the capital of the kingdom of Zhao.

A minister of the kingdom of Wei, Ji Liang, heard news of the upcoming attack while on a diplomatic trip to another country. He immediately turned his carriage around and headed back to Da Liang, his kingdom's capital, to talk as soon as possible with the king. He wanted the king to call off the invasion.

Unwashed and in wrinkled clothes, knowing he must hurry, Ji Liang requested an immediate audience with the king. The king of Wei, anxious to know why his minister had returned so soon, agreed to see him.

Ji Liang removed his hat and stood in front of the king, waiting for the king to speak first. With a worried expression, the king asked, "Why have you come back after making only half your journey?"

Ji Liang replied, "I have something of great importance to discuss with Your Majesty."

"Then please tell me straight away," said the king.

Ji Jiang looked down, hesitating before he spoke. "Let me tell you a story, a story that will make my message easy to understand." He cleared his throat and began.

"Today, when I stopped at an inn, I met a fellow traveler whose carriage was headed north, although he claimed that his destination was the kingdom of Chu."

Ji Liang continued. "I felt confused. The kingdom of Chu, as we both know, is located far to the south, so why wasn't he driving southward? Instead, he was driving his horses north. So I said to him, 'The kingdom of Chu lies to the south of Wei. So how do you plan to reach it by going north?'

"The fellow replied: 'My horses are powerful and very, very fast. They can run hundreds of miles a day.'

"Still puzzled, I said, 'Your horses may be fast, but this fact will not make the kingdom of Chu move from the south to the north.'

Ji Liang looked at the king and saw that he, too, was baffled by the man's actions. He went on, hoping that the point of the story would soon become clear. "Then the traveler patted his silk purse and said, 'Don't worry, Sir. I have plenty of money for my trip.'

"I asked more questions, still trying to make sense of the traveler's reaction. 'What's the use of having money for the trip,' I asked, 'if you're going in the wrong direction? This is simply not the way to the kingdom of Chu!'

"He replied, 'Ah, but my coachman is very skilled.'

"Perplexed and frustrated, I said to him, 'No matter what advantages you may have — fast horses, plenty of money, an excellent driver — if you insist on going to the north, it will just take you farther and farther from your destination.'"

Ji Liang drew a breath before finishing his story. "But in the end, sire, the traveler paid no attention to my advice. When he departed, he waved at me and then told his coachman to continue traveling north."

Ji Liang paused, clasped his hands behind his robes, looked at the king directly, and spoke with care. "I understand, Your Majesty, that you desire to rule all the kingdoms and gain their devotion, their respect, and their trust." Ji Liang paused again, letting his words take effect. "But I should like to ask," he continued, "how are respect and trust won?" The king raised his eyebrows, waiting to hear what his minister would say.

"They are won through the actions and the decisions you make," said Ji Liang. "Never will you gain the trust and respect of others by using your powerful army to invade a small and weak country."

Ji Liang went on: "Insisting on attacking the kingdom of Zhao contradicts your ultimate purpose, just as is the case with a man who insists on traveling north but hopes to reach a destination in the south."

The king nodded slowly and thoughtfully. Finding that he agreed with Li Jiang's argument, he called off the attack and left the kingdom of Zhao in peace.

齊人攫金 Qí Rén Jué Jīn

A Man from the Kingdom of Qi Snatches Gold

昔齊人有欲金者，清旦衣冠而之市，適鬻金者之所，因攫金而去。《列子·說符》

In the ancient kingdom of Qi, a lazy man wanted gold. He went into a gold store and, mesmerized by the gold, absentmindedly picked up a gold dish and left.

Retelling

Cóng qián zài qí guó, long ago, in the kingdom of Qi, there lived a lazy, aimless man. Because he never worked hard, he remained poor. Still, he longed to be rich and so he spent his time daydreaming, picturing himself atop mountains of gold and silver.

One day, inspired, he arose early in the morning, scrubbed himself clean, put on his best clothes, and walked to the market in search of gold. Dressed in his finest, he strolled down the street, inspecting here, examining there, lost in thought, wondering how he might manage to lay his hands on some gold.

After a time, a sparkling sign designating a store specializing in gold caught his eye. "What luck!" he said aloud. "This is just the place I wanted to find!" He smiled broadly and stepped inside.

He got no farther than a few steps. Stunned by the sight that greeted him, he could only stare in amazement. So much gold! In every shape and size, goblets and statues and jeweled ornaments—all made of pure gold! Gold covered the tables and walls: to the man from Qi, it was like waking up in a dream. He walked about the store in astonishment, slack-jawed. His fingers traced the gold figures of dragons, the glittering statues of goddesses, the jeweled necklaces and rings, the gold-leafed porcelain. He trembled with delight.

Then he spied a shallow golden dish with a fierce tiger embossed on it, with which he became utterly enchanted. The tiger looked alive, ready to pounce on its prey. The man from Qi held up the dish and turned it round and round, watching it reflect the light, feeling its power. Fascinated, he could not put it down and, without a second thought, wandered out of the store with it.

Soon after, the store owner saw that the golden dish was missing. He dashed outside.

"Stop the thief! A thief has stolen my gold dish!" Two officials patrolling nearby quickly ran after the man from Qi, who, lost in his admiration of the shimmering golden dish, hadn't gotten very far.

"You shameless thief!" one of the officials chastised him. "What made you think you could take the golden dish without paying?" Then they arrested him.

The man from Qi seemed to wake up just then and noticed the officials and the store owner glaring at him. He replied in confusion, "But . . . but, I didn't even notice that I'd taken the dish—all I could see was the gold."

刻舟求劍 Kè Zhōu Qíu Jiàn

Marking the Boat to Search for Your Sword in the River

楚人有涉江者，其劍自舟中墜於水，遽契其舟，曰："是吾劍之所從墜。"舟止，從其所契者入水求之。

舟已行矣，而劍不行，求劍若此，不亦惑乎？《呂不韋·呂氏春秋．察今》

A man from the kingdom of Chu was crossing a river. His sword fell out of the boat into the water, so he made a mark on the boat, saying, "This is the place my sword fell out." When the boat stopped, he jumped into the water for his sword, but he couldn't find his sword. The boat had moved but the sword had not.

Retelling

Gǔ shí hòu, in ancient times, during the Warring States Period, a man from the kingdom of Chu needed to cross a river and boarded a small boat to ferry him. He traveled with a priceless, double-edged sword embedded with precious stones and decorated with silver and gold scrollwork on the handle and sheath.

Other people joined him on the ferry, and because the sword hung conspicuously at his side, he quickly became the center of attention. The others gathered around to admire the extraordinary object. He felt proud, and drew the sword from its sheath so they could appreciate how sharp its edges were and how the jewels reflected the colors of the sky and water.

When the boat approached the middle of the river, a storm began to brew. The waves grew high and the wind strong. A powerful current seemed to grab the boat's hull, pushing it this way and that, while the waves made the boat pitch up and down. Man and sword almost fell in the river together, but at the last moment the man grabbed the edge of the boat and pulled himself upright. The sword, however, dropped into the middle of the river with a sound: *Pu tong!*

People gasped. Would there be any way to recover the sword after the storm died down? Perhaps then someone could dive into the river and find the sword. "Look at the landmarks on either side of the river at this exact spot," they advised him. "Then you'll be able to locate it again." But the man from Chu seemed unconcerned.

"Do not worry. I have my own way," he responded, without a trace of alarm. Then he took a small knife from his pocket and made a mark on the edge of the boat. "See?" he said. "This is the exact place where my sword fell out. When the boat reaches the shore,

I will search for it right below this mark. It will be easy to look near the riverbank, as the water is much shallower."

People began to snicker at his logic, but the man from Chu paid no attention to them.

The boat continued across the river, gradually moving downstream. When at last it arrived at the opposite bank, the man from Chu jumped into the water and began to look right below the mark on the edge of the boat. He searched here and there, feeling along the bottom of the river with his hands and turning over rocks, but he could not find his sword. He said to himself, "Isn't this the very place where my sword dropped into the water? Why can't I find it?"

His fellow travelers laughed at the sight of the swordsman's futile efforts. All but he understood that the boat had moved, while the sword had not.

掩耳盜鈴 Yǎn Ěr Dào Líng

范氏之亡也，百姓有得鐘者。欲負而走，則
鐘大不可負；以椎毀之，鐘況然有音。恐人
聞之而奪己也，遽掩其耳。 惡人聞之可也，
惡己自聞之，悖矣。《呂不韋·呂氏春秋·自知》

Plugging One's Ears While Stealing a Bell

After the nobleman Fan was defeated, a thief wanted to steal his bell by carrying it away on his back. The bell was huge, so he decided to break it into pieces with a hammer. The bell made a very loud noise. Fearing that other people would hear the sound and catch him, he plugged his ears. To neglect the fact that other people might hear the sound of the bell is understandable, but how ridiculous of him to cover up his own ears!

Retelling

Chūn qiū shí qī, during the Spring and Autumn Period, Zhi Bo, of the kingdom of Jin, battled with — and defeated — Fan, a rich nobleman. News of Fan's defeat spread quickly, and soon a thief showed up at the nobleman's house, hoping to take advantage of the situation.

As he slipped quietly into Fan's house, he spied a large bronze bell propped up in the corner of a room. Extremely pleased with this discovery, the thief decided to test the sound of the bell, for a perfectly cast bell makes a perfectly beautiful sound — soothing but very loud at the same time. He picked up a mallet that lay nearby and tapped the bell gently. The bell was large, though, and such a slight tap made no sound. He tapped a little harder, causing the bell to come alive with a lovely sound.

He decided he must have it. All he needed was a way to get it home. The thief pushed against the top of the bell, trying to tip it onto its side so he could roll it away. It wouldn't budge. He threw his whole body into it. Nothing happened. Breathless, he paused to think through this problem. Finally, he exclaimed, *"Yǒu le!* I've got an idea!" He decided to break the bell into a few moveable pieces and carry each home on his back.

Looking through the rubble of Fan's home, the thief found a hammer. He positioned himself in front of the bell, and, holding the hammer with both hands, swung it in a great arc, smack into the bell. *Dang!* The bell rang out loudly, loud enough for everyone in the countryside to hear.

The jarring sound even startled the thief. *"Zāo le!* That's bad!" He said. "Now everyone will know about the bell! What can I do?" Quickly, he reached up and covered his ears. The sound disappeared and a smile spread across his face. How easy it was to make the sound go away! "*Hǎo le!* That's perfect!" He wadded up some pieces of cotton and stuck one in each ear. Then he started to smash the bell into pieces.

"*Dang! Dang!*" the thief whacked at the bell, causing the sound to carry far and wide, but he was satisfied with his solution. The sound was muffled. "Now no one can hear the bell anymore," said the thief to himself, smiling.

But many people had heard the bell, and they came out of their homes in the surrounding villages. The thief, lurching away from Fan's home with a large piece of the bell on his back, was easily caught.

濫竽充數 Làn Yú Chōng Shù

齊宣王使人吹竽，必三百人。南郭處士請
為王吹竽。宣王悅之，廩食以數百人。宣王
死，湣王立。好一一聽之。處士逃。

《韓非子.內儲說上》

An Unskilled Musician Concealed in the Crowd

In the kingdom of Qi, King Xuan enjoyed listening to the yu, appreciating it most when it was played by a band of three hundred musicians. A man named Nan Guo applied to play the yu for King Xuan and secured a position. Nan Guo was treated well by the king, as were the other musicians. But King Xuan died, and Min, who enjoyed hearing the yu played solo, became king. Nan Guo fled.

Retelling

Chūn qīu shí qī, during the Spring and Autumn Period, in the kingdom of Qi, King Xuan loved to hear music. In particular, he enjoyed listening to a wind instrument called the *yu*. Quite often, as many as three hundred *yu* players gathered and performed for the king's pleasure, for he especially loved hearing the instrument played by a large band of musicians.

One day, a clever man, Nan Guo, heard of the king's fondness for large ensembles and realized that this might be an excellent opportunity for him to earn a good living. He waited until one of the king's musicians had fallen seriously ill and there was a vacancy in the royal orchestra. Without delay, Nan Guo went to the palace and boasted to King Xuan, "*Bì Xià*, Your Majesty, I am a famous artist of the *yu*. When I blow into my instrument, nothing remains unmoved—the butterflies and the birds flutter about to my rhythms, and even the beasts dance." Nan Guo gave the king an especially honeyed smile. "I am much in demand, but I would be willing to offer my talents exclusively for Your Majesty's enjoyment."

Taken in by Nan Guo's flowery promises, the king allowed him to join his large orchestra without even asking for an audition. Nan Guo was delighted. From then on, Nan Guo played his *yu* with the other musicians, all of whom were well paid, well fed, and comfortably housed in the king's expansive palace.

In reality, Nan Guo had lied to the king; he was no better than a beginner on the *yu*. But he watched carefully and precisely mimicked the other musicians. During a concert, he swayed with the melody when the other musicians swayed, tapped his toes to the rhythm when the others tapped their toes. He fit in perfectly. With so much splendid music surrounding him, not a soul suspected he was a fake, and he spent his days living in luxury.

Alas, nothing lasts forever, and Nan Guo's luck ran out soon enough. Just a few years later, King Xuan died, and the young prince of the kingdom, Min, inherited the throne. Like his father, King Min also enjoyed the *yu*, but, unlike his father, he preferred listening to the music played quietly, by a solo performer, so that he could appreciate each musician's unique style. He gave an order that the three hundred musicians were to play for him one by one, and that each man should choose his very favorite melody for the king's amusement.

That very night, Nan Guo crept out of the palace and fled.

塞翁失馬、 Sài Wēng Shī Mǎ

Old Man Sai Lost His Horse

夫禍福之轉而相告，其變難見也。近塞上之人，有善術者，馬無故亡而入胡。人皆弔之，其父曰："此何遽不為福乎？"居數月，其馬將胡駿馬而歸。人皆賀之，其父曰："此何遽不能為禍乎？"家富良馬，其子好騎，墮而折其髀。人皆弔之，其父曰："此何遽不為福乎？"居一年，胡人大入塞，丁壯者引弦而戰。近塞之人，死者十九。此獨以跛之故，父子相保。故福之為禍，禍之為福，化不可極，深不可測也。

《劉安·淮南子．人間訓》

Near the northern border there lived a man named Sai Weng, a fine rider and horse breeder. One day, his best horse ran away across the border for no reason at all. Everyone sympathized with him. "Perhaps this will turn out to be a blessing," said his elderly father.

After a few months, the horse came back, bringing along a fine horse from the north. Everyone congratulated the man.

"Perhaps this will soon turn out to be a cause of misfortune," said his father.

Since Sai Weng was well off and raised fine horses, his son was also fond of riding. But his son fell from a horse and broke his thighbone. Everyone felt sorry for him.

"Perhaps this will turn out to be a blessing," said Sai Weng's father.

One year later, the northern tribes invaded the border regions. All able-bodied young men had to take up arms and fight the intruders. As a result, nine out of ten young men in the region died. But the man's son did not have to fight because he was crippled, and so both the boy and his father survived. Thus, even this disaster brought happiness.

Retelling

Cóng qián, long ago, near the northern border of China, there lived a man named Sai Weng, a fine rider and skilled breeder of horses. One day, Sai Weng's best horse disappeared. Sai Weng traveled far across the northern areas of Xiong Nu in search of it. Unsuccessful, he returned home days later, alone and despondent. His favorite horse had simply vanished.

Neighbors came to console him, concerned that he might become ill with worry. "What a terrible, terrible tragedy!" said some of the village folk.

"How can he breed horses now? His best horse is gone," said others.

"This will be the sad end of his fine reputation!" they predicted.

Watching all the fretting and commotion, Sai Weng's elderly father shook his head slowly. "You never know," he said. "Perhaps this will turn out to be a blessing."

Although he was filled with doubt, Sai Weng listened closely to his father's words, turning them over in his mind and drawing comfort from them. The villagers, however, returned to their homes and continued their worried whispers.

A few months later, the lost horse wandered back into the village, and with him was a very fine horse from northern Xiong Nu. Word quickly spread of Sai Weng's great good fortune. Gathering round him, his neighbors thumped him on the back, full of congratulations. Sai Weng beamed.

But Sai Weng's elderly father watched calmly. After a while he remarked, "You never know. Perhaps this event will turn out to be the cause of misfortune."

Sai Weng listened to his father's words respectfully, while the villagers, admiring the newfound horse and its companion, ignored what the old man said. They celebrated late into the night.

For a time, Sai Weng's good luck held. His herd of horses grew larger, and his own family grew, too. His wife gave birth to a son just a few short years later, and he also came to love horses, especially riding them. The boy's favorite horse was the one from Xiong Nu, the horse that had come to the village as a mysterious gift of fortune. Each day at sunrise, the boy would dash outside to greet his horse, feed it some wild apples, and vault up onto its back.

One day, however, as the boy sped through a meadow on horseback, a mouse, frightened by the loud sound of hooves, scampered across his path. The horse startled. The boy flew off the saddle and landed full force on a rock, shattering his thighbone. His father found him a few hours later and gently carried him home.

Neighbors came to comfort the boy, for it looked as if his leg would never be strong again. To Sai Weng they poured out their sympathy, for the boy was his only child. But nearby sat Sai Weng's elderly father, who did not look so heartbroken. He dismissed the villagers' gloomy predictions. "You never know," he said. "Perhaps this will soon turn out to be a blessing."

One year later, northern tribes from Xiong Nu invaded the border regions. All able-bodied young men were ordered to take up arms and fight the intruders. None of the young men in the village escaped the draft, except for Sai Weng's son.

In the bloody battles that followed, nine out of ten young men in the region perished, and families were awash in grief. But, because he was crippled, Sai Weng's son did not have to fight, and both he and his family survived the war. A blessing had indeed accompanied the boy's misfortune.

愚公移山 Yú Gōng Yí Shān

太行王屋二山，方七百裡，高萬仞。本在冀
州之南，河陽之北。

北山愚公者，年且九十，面山而居。懲山北
之塞，出入之迂也。聚室而謀曰："吾與汝
畢力平險，指通豫南，達於漢陰，可乎？"
雜然相許其妻獻疑曰："以君之力，曾不能
損魁父之丘，如太行、王屋何？且焉置土
石？"雜曰："投諸渤海之尾，隱土之
北。"遂率子孫荷，擔者三夫，叩石墾壤，
箕畚運於渤海之尾。鄰人京城氏之孀妻有
遺男，始齔，跳往助之。寒暑易節，始一
返焉。

河曲智叟笑而止之曰："甚矣，汝之不惠。
以殘年余力，曾不能毀山之一毛，其如土石
何？"北山愚公長息曰："汝心之固，固不可
徹，曾不若孀妻弱子。雖我之死，有子存
焉；子又生孫，孫又生子；子又有子，子又有
孫；子子孫孫無窮匱也，而山不加增，何苦而
不平？"河曲智叟亡以應。

操蛇之神聞之，懼其不已也，告之於帝。帝感
其誠，命夸娥氏二子負二山，一厝朔東，一厝
雍南。自此，冀之南，漢之陰，無隴斷焉。

《列子·湯問篇》

NOTE: *As was the case with "A Frog in a Shallow Well," the original version of this story is also quite long. Again, rather than follow a full translation with an even longer version, we have chosen to retell the story in a way that elaborates only slightly on the original.*

Yu Gong Moved Mountains

Gǔ shí hòu, in ancient times, the mountains Taihang and Wangwu lay between the two states of Jizhou and Heyang, rising to a great height of thousands of *rèn*. Just north of these two mountains lived an old man named Yu Gong, meaning "foolish old man." He was nearly ninety years old.

Yu Gong's home faced the two mountains, and for years it had troubled him that the mountains blocked the way of the people in his city, forcing them to take an arduous and roundabout route whenever they went south. Yu Gong gathered his family together to discuss the matter.

"Let us do everything in our power to flatten these forbidding mountains so that there will be a direct route to the south of Jizhou," he proposed. "If we move these two mountains, everyone in our city will be able to reach the Han River easily. What do you say?"

Most applauded his suggestion, but his wife voiced her doubts. "You are old and weak and not even strong enough to remove a small hill! How can you tackle the giant mountains Taihang and Wangwu?" she asked. "Furthermore," she continued, "how could one get rid of so much earth and stone?"

Yu Gong was undeterred. "The Bohai Sea is vast and can contain it all. We can bring it to the sea," he said confidently.

His wife remained skeptical, but the rest of the family agreed to carry out Yu Gong's plan. Yu Gong, his three sons, and his grandsons were each capable of carrying a load on their shoulders, and so they set about their task. Day after day they broke up rocks and dug up mounds of earth that they transported in baskets to the edge of the Bohai Sea.

Yu Gong's neighbor, a widow by the name of Jingcheng, had a son who was just at the age when he was losing his silk teeth, or baby teeth. The young boy, full of energy, jumped at the chance to give the men a hand. And so from winter through summer they all worked together, returning home only once.

A man named Zhi Sou, meaning "wise old man," saw old Yu Gong working and laughed at him. Trying to dissuade Yu Gong, he said, "You are so foolish! You're far too old for this kind of work! You have so little strength left that you can't even destroy a blade of grass on the mountain, let alone move all this rock and stone!"

"*Nǐ cuò le!* You're wrong," said Yu Gong, heaving a patient sigh. "You are so stubborn that you do not see the situation clearly. Even my neighbor's little son understands our task better than you do." Zhi Sou looked doubtful, but Yu Gong continued. "My sons will continue my work after my death. 'Sons will have grandsons, and grandsons will have sons; sons and grandsons will continue without end,'" he explained. "Generation after generation, there will be no end to our effort, and we will succeed because the mountains, after all, can't grow any higher."

Yu Gong smiled. "Do you still believe I can't move the mountains?" he asked. Zhi Sou spoke no more about it.

Meanwhile, the God of Mountains had heard about Yu Gong's determination. He feared that Yu Gong would never stop digging, and so he reported the matter to the Heaven God. Upon learning of the story, the Heaven God was so greatly touched by Yu Gong's sincerity that he ordered another god to go down and take the two high mountains away.

From that time onward no mountain stood between the south of Jizhou and the banks of the Han River. The fruit of old Yu Gong's determination was success.

齒亡舌存 Chǐ Wáng Shé Cún

（樅）曰：“過故鄉而下車，子知之乎？”老子曰：“過故鄉而下車，非謂其不忘故邪？”常樅曰：“過喬木而下，子知之乎？”老子：“過喬木而下，非謂敬耶？”常樅曰：“嘻，是已。”張其口而示老子曰？“吾舌存乎？”老子曰：“然。”“吾齒存乎？”老子曰：“亡。”常樅曰：“子知之乎？”老子曰：“夫舌之存也，非以其剛耶？”常樅曰：“嘻！是已！天下之事已盡矣，無以復語子哉！”《劉向·說苑·敬慎》

The Teeth Are Gone, but the Tongue Remains

In the Autumn and Spring Period, Lao Tzu went to visit his teacher, Chang Zhong, shortly before his death, when the old master was very ill. Lao Tzu asked his teacher for a last word of wisdom.

Chang Zhong opened his mouth and asked, "Is my tongue there?"

Lao Tzu answered, "Yes!"

Then Chang Zhong asked, "Are there any teeth left?"

"None!" said Lao Tzu.

Chang Zhong asked his student for the reason. Lao Tzu answered, "The tongue is left because it is soft. The teeth are gone because they are hard."

Chang Zhong replied, "Yes! This explains everything in the world. I have nothing left to teach you."

Retelling

Chūn qiū shí qī, during the Spring and Autumn Period, Chang Zhong, who had taught the famous sage Lao Tzu, fell gravely ill. When Lao Tzu heard the news, he went to see his old teacher immediately.

When Lao Tzu arrived, he found Chang Zhong's house full of students. They spoke in soft voices, taking care to let the master rest. One of them led Lao Tzu to the teacher's bedside, in a dimly lit room. On the brink of death, Chang Zhong could barely turn his head to greet his finest pupil. Tenderly, Lao Tzu bent down so his teacher could see him more easily. He folded his teacher's hands within his own. "Teacher, how are you now? Are you comfortable enough?" he asked gently.

The old man held his gaze and gave a small nod. Lao Tzu smiled and gave a slight nod in reply. Chang Zhong closed his eyes. They stayed like that, in silence, for a long time. Chang Zhong's breath was irregular and difficult. Realizing that his teacher wouldn't last the night, Lao Tzu finally asked, "Master, I see you have become very, very ill. Do you not have some final teachings you would like to transmit to your many students?"

Chang Zhong opened his eyes. Lao Tzu could see that the answer was yes. Carefully, he helped the frail old man sit up a little, against some pillows, so he could address him face-to-face.

Lao Tzu said respectfully, "Teacher, I am ready to listen."

Chang Zhong began: "While passing your hometown, do you know why you are always supposed to get off your cart?"

Lao Tzu replied, "I get off my cart when passing by my hometown so as not to forget my old friends and my roots."

"Exactly," said Chang Zhong. Next he asked, "Do you know why I ask you to get off your horse when you pass by a large tree?"

Lao Tzu answered, "One pays respect to what is old. I always get off my horse when I approach a large tree because it reminds me that we must honor our elders as if they were our fathers."

Chang Zhong smiled, "*Shì*, yes, precisely right. You have learned well."

Some moments passed in thoughtful silence. Then Chang Zhong abruptly opened his mouth and pointed: "Lao Tzu, is my tongue there?"

Lao Tzu answered, "Yes!"

Then Chang Zhong asked, "Are there any teeth left?"

"*Bù*, no, none at all."

"Why is that?" Chang Zhong asked. Lao Tzu paused, pondering the question. At last he answered, "The tongue remains because it is soft. The teeth are gone because they are hard."

Chang Zhong replied, "Yes! Exactly! In all things, soft outlasts hard. As water will wear down any stone, no matter how firm, gentleness will always prove stronger than resistance over time." Chang Zhong smiled. "Learn from the Tao, from nature. The relationships among all things—whether human, rock, or tree—are summed up in this understanding."

He patted Lao Tzu's hand. "This teaching will guide your way in the world. I have nothing left to teach you."

With smiling eyes, Chang Zhong looked at his pupil one last time. Then the old teacher gently closed his eyes and took his rest.

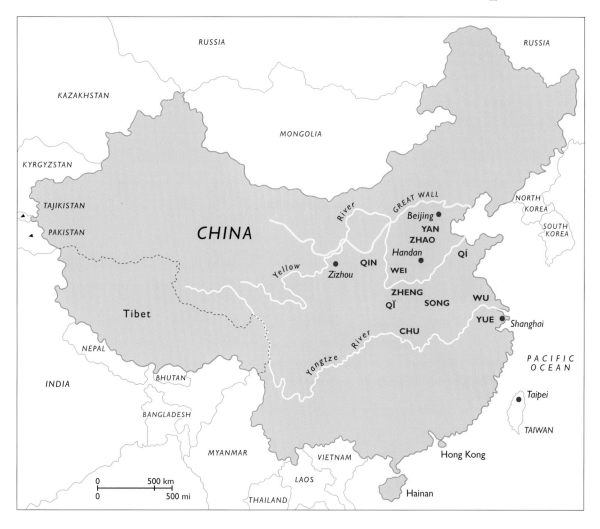

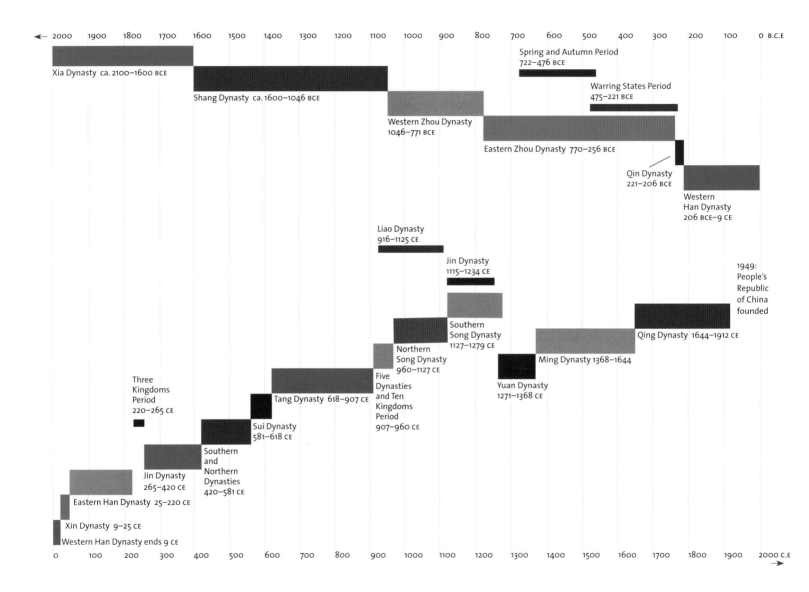

2000 1900 1800 1700 1600 1500 1400 1300 1200 1100 1000 900 800 700 600 500 400 300 200 100 0 B.C.E

Xia Dynasty ca. 2100–1600 BCE

Shang Dynasty ca. 1600–1046 BCE

Western Zhou Dynasty
1046–771 BCE

Eastern Zhou Dynasty 770–256 BCE

Spring and Autumn Period
722–476 BCE

Warring States Period
475–221 BCE

Qin Dynasty
221–206 BCE

Western
Han Dynasty
206 BCE–9 CE

Liao Dynasty
916–1125 CE

Jin Dynasty
1115–1234 CE

1949:
People's
Republic
of China
founded

Southern
Song Dynasty
1127–1279 CE

Northern
Song Dynasty
960–1127 CE

Qing Dynasty 1644–1912 CE

Five
Dynasties
and Ten
Kingdoms
Period
907–960 CE

Ming Dynasty 1368–1644

Three
Kingdoms
Period
220–265 CE

Tang Dynasty 618–907 CE

Yuan Dynasty
1271–1368 CE

Sui Dynasty
581–618 CE

Southern
and
Northern
Dynasties
420–581 CE

Jin Dynasty
265–420 CE

Eastern Han Dynasty 25–220 CE

Xin Dynasty 9–25 CE

Western Han Dynasty ends 9 CE

0 100 200 300 400 500 600 700 800 900 1000 1100 1200 1300 1400 1500 1600 1700 1800 1900 2000 C.E

English speakers often have a hard time learning to pronounce Chinese correctly. Mandarin contains sounds that do not occur in English, and what the Chinese hear as two different sounds can seem indistinguishable to speakers of English. (For example, both pinyin *ch* and *q* are similar to the English *ch*.) Nonetheless, by following a few simple guidelines, you can achieve a reasonable approximation of the Chinese.

c	ts	hi**ts**
ch	the *ch* in chin, but curl your tongue up and back	
h	a rough *ch*, as in the Scottish *loch*	
q	ch	**ch**urch
x	sh, but with the tongue curled up, as in the German *Ich*	
z	dz	be**ds**
zh	a sound somewhere between *j* and *ch*, similar to the *g* in mer**g**er	
a	ah	**fa**ther
ai	aye	**eye**
ao	ow	h**ow**
e	uh	h**u**rry
ei	eiy	m**ay**
i	ee	s**ee**n (but at the end of a word is closer to the *i* in b**i**t)
ia	ee-ah	**ya**rn
ian	ee-en	**yen**

iao	ee-ow	m**eow**
ie	ee-eh	**ye**s
iu	ee-oh	**yeo**man
o	oh, but pronounced back in the throat	
ou	oh	d**ou**gh
ong	the oo in **foo**t, with an ng	
u	oo	r**u**ler
ua	oo-ah	**wa**ter
uai	oo-eye	**why**
ui	oo-ay	**way**

Unlike English, Chinese is a tonal language. Mandarin has four tones (although some Chinese dialects, such as Cantonese, have more). These are:

high	ā	an even, high pitch, much as if the sound were being sung
rising	á	the sound rises from mid-level to high
dipping	ǎ	descends from mid-level to low, with a slight rise at the end
falling	à	a short sound, with a quick descent from high to low

In what follows, we have provided phonetic equivalents for Chinese words and phrases. For producing the tones, the best advice we can offer is this. First, speak the word out loud, using the phonetic pronunciation provided. Second, "draw" the accompanying tone in the air, using your finger. Finally, say the word again phonetically, while also drawing the tone in the air, and have your voice follow the motion of your finger.

Here is a list of the words and phrases that occur in the stories:

bì xià	bee sheeyah	Your Majesty
bù	boo	no
bú duì	boo duwei	wrong, incorrect
bù hǎo le	boo how luh	It is bad!
cóng qián	tsong chien	long ago
cóng qǐan zài qí guó	tsong chien dzai chee gwo	long ago, in the kingdom of Qi (Qí)
cóng qián zài sòng guó	tsong chien dzai song gwo	long ago in the kingdom of Song
chūn qiū shí qī	chwun chi-yo shuh chee	during the Spring and Autumn Period
dǒu lì	doe li	the hat worn by Chinese peasants
gǔ shí hòu	goo shuh ho	in ancient times
hǎo	how	okay, good
hǎo le	how luh	okay
hēi, yǒu le	hey, yo luh	Oh, I've got an idea!
hèn	hun	a sound of disdain
kuài	kwai	Hurry up!
lǐ	lee	a Chinese unit of distance, which has varied considerably over time but now has a standardized length of half a kilometer (500 meters)
méi shén me	may shuh muh	It's nothing special
nǐ cuò le	nee tswoh luh	You're wrong!
rèn	ren	an ancient Chinese unit used for measuring height; one *ren* is about 1.8 meters

shén me?	shen muh	What?
shì	shi	yes
tài hǎo le	tai how luh	Wonderful!
wǒ yǒu le	wo-oh yo-oh luh	I have an idea!
yí?	ee	What's going on?
yǒu le	yo-oh luh	I've got an idea!
zāo le	dzao luh	Oh no! That's bad!
zhàn guó shí qī	jahn gwo shuh chee	in the Warring States Period

China today remains a breathtaking blend. It is a merging of ancient wisdom and an increasingly modern spirit that is infused with a palpable energy—an energy born of the determination of the world's largest national population to feed, house, and educate itself. When you travel through China, just as when you travel through these stories, you will encounter a mix of influences rather than distinct separations between religious and philosophical traditions. For example, the summit of Mount Tai—regarded by Taoists as the holiest of all mountains—has been a sacred spot for over three thousand years. In 219 BCE, Shi Huang, the first emperor to unite China, chose Mount Tai as the site for his consecration, and subsequent emperors worshiped Heaven and Earth at the summit and base of the mountain. If you climb the 7,700 stone steps up Mount Tai, you will pass by many Taoist shrines lining the route, but you will also find Buddhist sūtras inscribed in cliffs and even under waterfalls. At a souvenir shop along the way, you might come across a statue of the Buddha sitting next to a statue of the folk deity Cai Shen, the god of wealth, both adorned with generous offerings of incense and flowers. At an inn near the summit, you might purchase a scroll decorated with a beautiful ink-brush painting of the female deity Guan Yin, the Buddhist embodiment of compassion (whom Taoists also worship), along with a copy of *The Analects of Confucius* and a book bag inscribed with the Maoist slogan "Work for the people."

One often hears that China has three principal religions, Taoism, Confucianism, and Buddhism, but the lines between them are far from sharply drawn. Especially on the level of everyday religious observance, they overlap, sometimes quite extensively. Each has influenced the others, and all have absorbed elements of folk religion, as well as ideas from other schools of thought. What follows is a very brief account of the most important philosophical and religious traditions that have shaped Chinese culture and that underlie the stories in this book.

THE ONE HUNDRED SCHOOLS OF THOUGHT

The One Hundred Schools of Thought is a name associated with the period from 770 to 221 BCE, an era traditionally subdivided into the Spring and Autumn Period (770–476 BCE) and the Warring States Period (475–221 BCE). Although the Eastern Zhou Dynasty claimed the imperial throne, China consisted of an assortment of small kingdoms, each with its own ruler, and power was fragmented. The lack of centralized control may have contributed to the intellectual ferment characteristic of these years, which are often celebrated as the Golden Age of Chinese philosophy. The era was rich with itinerant philosophers and sages, who traveled from kingdom to kingdom hoping to find employment as royal counselors.

Confucius and his famous pupil, Mencius, lived during this time, as did Zhuangzi (Chuang Tzu), to whom one of Taoism's most important texts is ascribed. So did Mozi (Mo Tzu), who taught that individuals must love one another equally and must assume personal responsibility for their moral development. His egalitarian spirit, coupled with his distaste for ritual and the veneration of ancestors, set him up in opposition to Confucian thinkers, while his empiricism stood in contrast to the mystical element in Taoist thought.

A school of political philosophy known as legalism also developed during this period. Legalist thinkers advocated the rule of law, believing that people were inherently foolish and corrupt and must be kept in line by the threat of punishment. To govern effectively, a leader must have absolute power over his subjects and cannot afford to be too benevolent. At the same time, legalists generally supported a system of meritocracy, arguing that advancement should be based on performance rather than social position. Not surprisingly, the Machiavellian character of legalist theories appealed to many of China's emperors. Although the school of legalism eventually fell into disfavor, Confucian thinkers incorporated some of its ideas, and legalist influences continued to be visible in Chinese statecraft. Even Mao Zedong openly admired certain legalist principles, for example, the use of reward and punishment as a way of managing the civil bureaucracy.

TAOISM

Taoism is deeply intertwined in China's history and culture. Although Confucianism has had a greater impact on Chinese social structure, most would agree that the concept of the Tao, or the Way, is the centerpiece of Chinese philosophy and religious practice.

Invisible but pervasive, the Tao (道 *dào*) is the energy that underlies and sustains the universe, the force that keeps the universe in balance. As such, the Tao is intimately linked to nature, which is seen as its quintessential expression. As human beings, we are endowed with will, and, in an effort to shape the world to our satisfaction, we frequently exert our will in ways that run contrary to the Tao. This produces discord and discontent. Instead, we must learn how to align ourselves with Tao—to exist in harmony with the natural flow of creation.

The principal text of Taoism is the *Tao Te Ching* (more correctly transliterated *Daodejing*). Along with the *Bible*, the *Tao Te Ching* is one of the most frequently translated books in the world. A relatively brief text, it consists primarily of aphoristic statements that are often quite poetic but whose meaning is not always straightforward. The text is divided into two sections, the *Tao Ching* and the *Te Ching*. *Te* (德 *dé*), which means "virtue" or "integrity," refers to an inner strength of character, the quality that endows a person with moral power. *Te* can be understood as the active expression of the Tao in a human being—its living manifestation. *Ching* is the Chinese term for "scripture" or "classic," and so *Tao Te Ching* roughly means "Scriptures About the Way and About Virtue." The *Tao Te Ching* is intended to teach people how to exist in balance with the Tao and draw on its energy.

According to tradition, the *Tao Te Ching* was written in the sixth century BCE and is the work of Laozi (Lao Tzu), an honorific name meaning the "Old Master." Laozi is traditionally regarded as the "founder" of Taoism, but whether such a person ever actually existed remains a matter of debate. Similarly, evidence suggests that the *Tao Te Ching* was composed somewhat later, perhaps in the fourth century BCE, although its date is equally a subject of dispute. In all likelihood, the *Tao Te Ching* is a compilation of long-standing oral traditions that were finally written down.

Another work that has had an enormous influence on Taoist thought is the *Zhuangzi* (or *Chuang Tzu*). As we have it today, the text is clearly the product of many hands, although its first seven chapters (the "inner chapters") are said to have been written by a sage named Zhuangzi, who lived in the fourth century BCE. In contrast to the aphoristic style of the *Tao Te Ching*, the *Zhuangzi* prefers to use stories to convey its ideas. Zhuangzi favored withdrawal from the world and the individual pursuit of enlightenment, believing that each person must find his or her own path to the truth. In his view, the world does not need to be governed. Provided we do not interfere in its operation, it will find its own natural order and balance.

Of critical importance to Taoism is the concept of *wu wei* (無為 *wú wéi*), which literally means "without action." The sense of the term is commonly summed up in the paradoxical phrase *wei wu wei*, "action without action," and *wu wei* is often translated as "effortless action." Rather than rely on our will, which causes us to become self-centered and inflexible, we need to attune ourselves to the Tao and discover the strength that lies in suppleness. Through the practice of *wu wei*, we learn to stop behaving in ways that obstruct the Tao. As our resistance diminishes, we find a natural power or energy, much like that of water, which is soft and shapeless and yielding and yet can wear away mountains and etch patterns in stone. Zhuangzi argued that the practice of *wu wei* culminates in a state of pure receptiveness, one in which judgment and preconception are suspended. In this state, one is able to perceive the world clearly and directly, and its essential nature is revealed.

Taoist ethical teachings are founded on the Three Jewels, or Three Treasures. The first of these is compassion or kindness (*cí*), the cultivation of a gentle, loving attitude toward the world and its creatures. The second is moderation or restraint (*jiǎn*), which teaches us to rein in our desires and live in a way that is simple and uncluttered. The third is humility or the absence of ambition, in which we let go of the desire to be the first or the most important. It is the lack of humility that fuels competition and strife.

As a religion, Taoism may seem a bewildering amalgam of ideas and practices. A distinction was at one point made between Taoism as a religion (*dàojiāo*) and Taoism as a school of philosophy (*dàojiā*), but the two are so difficult to separate that the distinction has largely been abandoned. The formal pantheon is composed of an array of deities, hierarchically arranged, on the model of the Chinese imperial bureaucracy. The details of the arrangement are not fixed, however, and specific deities vary in popularity from region to region. In addition, Taoist practice incorporates a great many elements of folk religion, including the worship of nature spirits and ancestor spirits. There is a priesthood, although not all Taoists avail themselves of priestly services. The *Tao Te Ching* is regarded as the seminal text of Taoism, and yet the Taoist canon contains nearly fifteen hundred different texts. It is not easy, then, to identify a specific set of practices that are common to all (or even most) Taoists. Be they mystics or statesmen, however, Taoists share the same basic aspiration: to embrace the rhythm of the Tao and tap into its mysterious wisdom and harmony.

CONFUCIANISM

Whereas Taoism focuses on the individual's attunement to the natural realm, Confucianism is concerned instead with the individual's place in society. Kong Fuzi, known in the West as Confucius, was China's foremost moral philosopher. He lived from 551 to 479 BCE, during the unsettled times of the Warring States Period. Like the many other itinerant sages of the period, Confucius roamed the countryside, attracting disciples as he searched for a ruler who would implement his ideas on governance. Finding much in his travels that distressed him, he devoted himself to inspiring people to be virtuous.

Confucius linked virtuous behavior to traditional roles and hierarchies, arguing that an individual's moral development takes place within the context of family and other relationships. He believed that the practice of everyday ritual observances, including rules of etiquette, encourages people to internalize the principles of right action. Of paramount importance to Confucius was filial piety—the reverence of children for their parents and elders—which he viewed as the guiding principle of morality and social harmony. This reverence was due as much to one's ancestors as to the living.

Critical to the practice of rites was the existence of a clearly established social hierarchy, for an individual's duties depend on his or her status relative to others. Confucius envisaged a world in which a knowledge of duty, an attitude of benevolence, and adherence to social convention would govern action, which would result in a peaceful, well-ordered society.

The philosopher Mencius (Mengzi), who lived in the fourth century BCE, was the chief interpreter of Confucian thought. According to Mencius, human beings are innately endowed with virtue but are corrupted by evil influences and so must work to recover the moral goodness with which they were born. Perhaps the supreme virtue in the Confucian system is *ren* (仁), or "humaneness," although the term can also be translated as "perfect goodness" or "benevolence." *Ren* is closely related to the golden rule of reciprocity: what you do not wish for yourself, do not do to others. In Confucian political theory, a virtuous ruler possesses *ren* and therefore always acts with deep concern for his subjects. A selfish and pitiless ruler, one devoid of *ren*, risks losing the Mandate of Heaven, and hence the right to rule.

Although Confucius had enormous respect for the learned elite, he taught that all people were capable of pursuing knowledge and carrying out their responsibilities toward others with sincerity and goodness. He had little use for the aristocratic notion that birth into a noble family automatically confers honor and makes someone a "gentleman." Instead, much like the legalists, Confucius favored a meritocracy, in which honor and advancement would depend on one's excellence of character. This idea gave rise to a system of imperial examinations, intended in part to assess moral worth, that candidates for government office were obliged to pass. The system had its inception under the Han Dynasty (206 BCE–220 CE) and has continued into modern times.

Confucian tradition, with its emphasis on etiquette and social hierarchy, duty, and the cultivation of moral virtue, may seem antithetical to Taoism, which encourages spontaneity, a love of paradox, and individual freedom from societal conventions. Rather than see the two as opposed, however, the inclusive Chinese spirit has preferred to view them as complementary. Throughout the centuries, many Chinese have adhered to Confucian values and rituals as the basis for family and public life, while turning to Taoist ideas and practices as a foundation for their private spiritual life.

Confucianism has no priesthood and no "church," nor do Confucians worship a specific deity or group of deities. Thus, in the eyes of Western scholars especially, Confucianism is often said to be a philosophy rather than a religion, even though the distinction between the two tends not to apply in China. Regardless of the label we choose to affix to it, however, Confucian doctrine remained the moral foundation of Chinese society, and of many other East Asian societies, for over two millennia. In the twentieth century, the revolutionary Chinese communist government attempted to rid Chinese society of its Confucian mind-set, which it viewed as a hindrance to modernization. Especially during the Cultural Revolution of the 1970s, the practice of Confucianism was actively suppressed. But traditional habits of the mind and heart are not easy to dislodge, and the past few decades have seen a renewed interest in Confucianism on the Chinese mainland.

BUDDHISM

Unlike Taoism and Confucianism, Buddhism did not originate in China. Its founder was Siddhārtha Gautama, a prince born in northern India in the sixth century BCE. Tradition has it that the Buddha, as he later came to be known, abandoned his privileged existence when he discovered the existence of suffering in the world and took up the life of a wandering ascetic. At first he practiced severe forms of self-mortification, but, finding these fruitless, he eventually accepted some food and then sat down beneath a tree to meditate. This more moderate approach culminated in his enlightenment, and the notion of a Middle Way between extremes remains central to Buddhist teaching.

"Buddha" means "the awakened one," a name that implies an arising from the sleep of ignorance to an understanding of the true nature of reality. After his enlightenment, the Buddha taught for forty-five years, attracting many disciples.

At the time of his enlightenment, the Buddha gained insight into the Four Noble Truths, which are fundamental to Buddhist teaching. The first of these is the recognition that suffering is inherent in existence. The second teaches that suffering arises from certain causes. The third states that liberation from suffering is possible, and the fourth lays out the Eightfold Path, which is the means to this release. The first three steps of the Eightfold Path pertain to ethical conduct, the second three are concerned with mental discipline, and the final two have to do with the development of insight or wisdom. The diligent pursuit of these practices will eventually culminate in liberation from suffering. Especially at the outset, Buddhism was primarily a monastic religion. Lay people could earn merit by behaving ethically and by giving alms to monks, but the ideal life entailed a retreat from worldly affairs.

Over the course of time, disagreements arose concerning various points of doctrine, including the true nature of enlightenment. This led to the development of a new branch of Buddhism, called the Mahāyāna, or "Great Vehicle." In contrast to the more conservative tradition—the Theravāda, or "Doctrine of the Elders"—Mahāyāna Buddhism accepted a much greater number of texts as authoritative. Of paramount importance in Mahāyāna tradition is the notion of a bodhisattva—someone who attains enlightenment but, out of compassion for those still trapped in suffering, chooses to remain in the world as a teacher. Although Buddhism is basically nontheistic, Mahāyānists worship bodhisattvas much in the way that Christians revere saints.

In the first century CE, Buddhism began arriving in China, along with commercial goods, following the trade routes from northern India. At first Buddhism was seen as a religion of foreigners and, because Taoist terms were used for early translations of Buddhist texts into Chinese, was also taken to be a variant of Taoism.

At least initially, Chinese literati and bureaucrats, for whom Confucian values were paramount, were not terribly interested in a religion that encouraged individuals to renounce family and social life in order to devote themselves to the pursuit of enlightenment. To survive on Chinese soil, Buddhism had to reconcile its teachings with prevailing Chinese custom and belief. Thus, for example, the argument was made that one who attains enlightenment brings honor to his family. All the same, while Buddhism found a following among Chinese peasants, official support for the religion was slow to come, as well as sporadic, depending largely on the predilection of particular rulers.

Mahāyāna Buddhist philosophy was developing at the time that Buddhism was introduced in China, and so what the Chinese were exposed to in the early centuries was not a single creed of Buddhism but a large array of Buddhist beliefs and practices. Especially important in China is Pure Land Buddhism, a Mahāyāna school whose origins lie in India but whose evolution took place primarily in China, starting in the fifth century CE. Pure Land Buddhism teaches that salvation can be attained simply by worshiping the bodhisattva Amitābha, for this will lead to rebirth in a paradise called the Pure Land, in which one cannot fail to achieve enlightenment. Because Pure Land Buddhism did not require that one take up the life of a monk, and because it made enlightenment readily available to everyone, no matter how humble, it contributed significantly to Buddhism's growth in popularity.

Two other schools of Mahāyāna Buddhism evolved in China. One of these was Chan Buddhism, in which the emphasis fell on meditative practices rather than devotion. Although Chan Buddhism was never as influential in China as Pure Land Buddhism, it was exported to Japan, where it is known as Zen Buddhism. The other school, the Vajrayāna, was founded on a body of esoteric texts, or tantras, which taught adepts how to channel physical and mental energy so as to achieve intense powers of concentration, which were believed to hasten enlightenment. The Vajrayāna school took root in Tibet and is often called Tibetan Buddhism. Today, most Chinese Buddhists practice some form of Pure Land, often incorporating elements of Chan philosophy, and Buddhism remains a vibrant force in Chinese spiritual life.

———————

Since the beginnings of Chinese history, religion in China has been remarkably pluralistic. Ultimately, it is impossible to separate "formal" Chinese religion from folk traditions and mythology. Taoism, Confucianism, and Buddhism alike have incorporated the worship of local guardian deities, spirit cults, and the veneration of ancestors, as well as any number of festivals, divination practices, and household rituals. Myths about benevolent rulers of the distant past have found their way into Confucian political philosophy, folk saints or deities appear in the guise of Buddhist bodhisattvas or figures in the Taoist pantheon, and traditional folktales are preserved in Buddhist philosophical treatises and in the Taoist canon. Even though folk deities appear in only two of the stories in this anthology ("A Monkey Fishing Up the Moon" and "Yu Gong Moved Mountains"), one cannot underestimate the degree to which ancient myths, local legends, and age-old ritual practices have permeated Chinese religious life. While such cross-pollination is by no means unique to China, Chinese religious culture has proved itself unusually synthetic. As the well-known symbol of yin and yang suggests, the world is the sum of opposing forces that balance each other, in a spirit of harmony.

杞人憂天 Qǐ Rén Yōu Tiān

A MAN IN QI WORRIES THAT THE SKY WILL FALL

This story is from a text called the *Liezi*, which, like the *Tao Te Ching* and the writings of Zhuangzi, is regarded as one of the classic works of Taoism. The *Liezi* is attributed to Lie Yukou, who is said to have lived in the fifth century BCE, during the time of the One Hundred Schools of Thought. The story illustrates the Taoist principle of *wu wei*, which teaches us to avoid useless action. The Chinese tell this story to remind each other that if we look for something to be annoyed at or worried about, we can always find it. So do not seek worries! It is also used to warn people that the mind easily forms bad habits that can be difficult to break and to encourage them to be more flexible and open-minded.

Location: Feudal state of Qi (杞 Qǐ), modern Qi county, Henan province, east-central China

	Pinyin	*Pronunciation*	*Definition*
杞	qǐ	chee-ee	the name of a feudal state; a willow
人	rén	ren	a man; a person or people
憂	yōu	yo	worried
天	tiān	tee-en	sky; heaven; day

守株待兔 Shǒu Zhū Dài Tù

WAITING FOR A HARE BY A TREE STUMP

This idiom is extremely common in Chinese society. Children learn it in primary school, and people use it to make the point that, with rare exception, we have to work in order to succeed. The story is from the *Hanfeizi*, the collected works of a philosopher named Han Feizi, who lived in the third century BCE. He was one of the founders of the school known as legalism, which upholds the rule of law as the basis for a well-ordered society. Han Feizi viewed the Tao as a natural law that everyone and everything must obey. Similarly, the ideal ruler should function like an inevitable force of nature, imposing laws by which others must abide. There was a renewed interest in legalism under the rule of the Communist leader Mao Zedong, who admired some of the strict principles that the philosophy lays forth.

Legalist thinkers emphasized the importance of discipline. The story pokes fun at those who, like the farmer, simply wait for success to arrive without paying for it by hard work. When these stories were first recorded, however, no hard and fast lines existed among philosophical schools, and the story can also be given a Taoist reading. Anyone who understands the Tao would know that nature can't be counted on to produce a strange accident, such as a hare colliding with a tree stump, every day.

Location: Kingdom of Song, modern Henan province, east-central China

	Pinyin	*Pronunciation*	*Definition*
守	shǒu	sho-oh	to guard
株	zhū	joo	a tree trunk
待	dài	dai	to wait; to intend to do
兔	tù	tu	a rabbit; a hare

揠苗助長 Yà Miáo Zhù Zhǎng

PULLING UP SPROUTS TO HELP THEM GROW

Parents and teachers invoke this *chengyu* when someone tries to rush things or hurry a process along in a way that runs contrary to its nature. In particular, the story is often heard when someone pushes a child to excel too quickly. As some people see it, especially because of the hardships of the past century, parents in China today tend to place excessively high expectations on their children and pressure them to succeed. Although Confucian tradition encourages study and diligent effort, the story reminds us of the need for moderation.

The idiom and story are attributed to the philosopher Mencius, who lived from 382 to 304 BCE, during the Warring States Period. Mencius was one of Confucius's most important students and is given credit for the widespread dissemination of Confucian ideas. But the story has a distinctly Taoist flavor. The farmer, who wants to force something to happen in a way that isn't natural, fails to acknowledge the principle of *wu wei*. His actions conflict with the Tao, which brings him sorrow.

Location: Kingdom of Song, modern Henan province, east-central China

	Pinyin	*Pronunciation*	*Definition*
揠	yà	yah	to eradicate; to pull up
苗	miáo	meow	a sprout
助	zhù	ju	to help; to assist
長	zhǎng	jah-ong	to grow; to develop

盲人摸象 Máng Rén Mō Xiàng

BLIND MEN TOUCH AN ELEPHANT

The Chinese commonly use this *chengyu* to describe a person who sees only one part of an issue rather than the whole truth. As the presence of an elephant suggests, the story appears to have originated in India and probably arrived in China with Buddhism. In China, the story is found in the *Chuan Deng Lu*, a text composed during the eleventh and twelfth centuries CE and intended to popularize Buddhism. The story teaches that all viewpoints are partial. Those who have not yet achieved enlightenment are like the blind men. Still trapped in delusion (*moha*), they persist in imposing this or that "correct" interpretation on reality.

Location: Originally set in India but popular in north-central China, modern Shaanxi, Henan, and Shanxi provinces

	Pinyin	*Pronunciation*	*Definition*
盲	máng	mahng	blind
人	rén	ren	a man; a person or people
摸	mō	mo	to feel with the hand; to touch
象	xiàng	sheeang	an elephant

磨杵成針 Mó Chǔ Chéng Zhēn

SHARPENING AN IRON BAR INTO A NEEDLE

This idiom and its story appear in a short text written by Zhu Mo, who lived during the Southern Song Dynasty (1127–1279 CE). A keen student of geography, Zhu Mo was also the author of *fangyu*, short treatises or pamphlets produced with the goal of attracting people to a particular area of the country. Most Song Dynasty scholars were Confucian, and the story Zhu Mo tells has a definite Confucian flavor. In contrast to Taoist thinkers, who placed little emphasis on worldly success, Confucius taught that people should study hard so that they could enter government service and thereby improve their situation in life. Today, the Chinese use this *chengyu* to remind others that success is the result of patience and dedicated effort and to urge them to persevere.

Location: Mei county, modern Sichuan province, south-central China

	Pinyin	*Pronunciation*	*Definition*
磨	mó	mo	to sharpen; to grind; to delay; a hardship
杵	chǔ	choo-u	a pestle; to poke
成	chéng	chung	to become; to turn into; to finish; to accomplish
針	zhēn	jen	a needle

鷸蚌相爭 Yù Bàng Xiāng Zhēng

THE FIGHT BETWEEN A SNIPE AND AN OYSTER

This story was taken from the *Intrigues of the Warring States* (*Zhan Guo Ce*), a rich compendium of historical tales that is also a literary gem. Its original authorship is unknown, although portions of the text may date back at least to the early third century BCE. The text as we have it, which is clearly not the work of a single person, was compiled and edited by Liu Xiang, a famous Confucian scholar who lived from 77 to 6 BCE, during the Western Han Dynasty (206 BCE–9 CE). Confucian morality emphasized benevolence and harmony, but it also encouraged people to be practical. If the only way to prosper is to reach out to an enemy and agree to stop fighting, then why prolong the battle? When the snipe fought with the oyster, both forgot about their common enemy, human beings, and so became vulnerable. Their tragedy warns people that unless they cooperate and help each other whenever they can, everyone will suffer. The Chinese also tell this story to remind those who are caught up in a conflict that they may be giving others an opportunity at their own expense.

Location: Kingdom of Zhao and kingdom of Yan, modern Hebei province, northeast China

	Pinyin	*Pronunciation*	*Definition*
鷸	yù	ew	a common snipe
蚌	bàng	bahng	an oyster; a mussel
相	xiāng	sheeang	one another; mutually
爭	zhēng	jung	to struggle; to fight

邯鄲學步 Hán Dān Xué Bù

STUDYING HOW TO WALK IN HANDAN

The story was taken from the "Autumn Floods" chapter of the *Zhuangzi*, a collection of tales and parables that is not only central to Taoist philosophy but is considered one of the great masterpieces of Chinese literature. Zhuangzi was a philosopher who, according to tradition, lived in the fourth century BCE. He was something of a skeptic and liked to poke fun at rationalists such as Confucius. In this story, he teaches us that learning is not a matter of imitation but of finding the way that is natural. If we ignore what is natural (the Tao), we eventually get so out of balance that we are effectively crippled, like the young man in the story, who in the end could only crawl. Nowadays, the *chengyu* is applied to people who copy others unthinkingly. Until we gain sufficient self-insight, it suggests, we will sacrifice our innate abilities as we struggle to be someone other than who we are.

Location: Town of Shouling, in the kingdom of Yan, and Handan, the capital of the kingdom of Zhao, modern Hebei province, northeast China

	Pinyin	*Pronunciation*	*Definition*
邯鄲	hán dān	hahn-dahn	a place name
學	xué	shooeh	to learn; to study; a science
步	bù	bu	a step; to walk; the stages in a process

坎井之蛙 Kǎn Jǐng Zhī Wā

A FROG IN A SHALLOW WELL

Like the previous story, this one is also taken from the *Zhuangzi*. In the story, the frog's view of the world is very circumscribed—but the problem isn't really that the frog's experience is limited: everyone's is. In his ignorance, however, he believes otherwise. He assumes that the little he knows is all there is. The turtle, who dwells in an ocean as infinite as the Tao, is wise and calm; the frog is excitable and self-important. The story is a beautiful illustration of Zhuangzi's warning that it is foolish to try to understand the unlimited—the Tao, the true nature of reality—by means of human knowledge, which is inherently finite. The expression "a frog in a shallow well" is used nowadays to refer to someone who seldom ventures beyond his or her small area of expertise or to suggest that someone is narrow-minded.

Location: None specified

	Pinyin	*Pronunciation*	*Definition*
坎	kǎn	kahn	a pit, a hole, a snare, a danger; a crisis
井	jǐng	jee-ing	a well
之	zhī	je	(possessive marker)
蛙	wā	wah	a frog

狐假虎威 Hú Jiǎ Hǔ Wēi

THE FOX BORROWS THE TIGER'S POWER

This is another story from the *Intrigues of the Warring States*, compiled and edited in the first century BCE by the Confucian scholar Liu Xiang, who was enormously fond of history and storytelling. Although to someone from the West, the story might seem to praise the fox for its resourcefulness and cunning, the Chinese interpret the story quite differently. The fox is seen as too clever, a dishonest manipulator, and so is judged as unethical. The tiger, however, is viewed as noble, straightforward, and honest. The *chengyu* is used in a derogatory manner to refer to people who take advantage of the protection of others and bully the weak. For example, some use it to criticize government bureaucrats who push people around, secure in the knowledge that behind them looms a strong "tiger."

Location: Kingdom of Chu, modern Hunan and Hubei provinces, south-central China

	Pinyin	*Pronunciation*	*Definition*
狐	hú	hoo	a fox
假	jiǎ	jee-ah	fake; false; to borrow
虎	hǔ	hoo-oo	a tiger
威	wēi	way	power; might; prestige

自相矛盾 Zì Xiāng Máo Dùn

HIS SPEAR AGAINST HIS SHIELD

This is another story from the legalist philosopher Han Feizi, who lived in the third century BCE, during the Warring States Period, when China was still fractured into numerous competing kingdoms. The story suggests that we should be skeptical of those who make grand claims or a show of power, for such people are sometimes trying to conceal weakness behind their boasts. This *chengyu* is often heard when a person says or does something that doesn't appear to be consistent with what the person has said or done earlier.

Location: Kingdom of Chu, modern Hunan and Hubei provinces, south-central China

	Pinyin	*Pronunciation*	*Definition*
自	zì	dzi	self; oneself; from; since
相	xiāng	sheeang	one another; mutually
矛	máo	mao	a spear; a lance
盾	dùn	doon	a shield

鄭人置履　Zhèng Rén Zhì Lǚ

A MAN FROM THE KINGDOM OF ZHENG BUYS SHOES

Like the previous story, this one also appears in the *Hanfeizi*, the collected works of the legalist philosopher Han Feizi, who lived during the third century BCE. It may seem an odd story, but when you think about it, you may realize that many people do the same thing as the man from Zheng. They place their faith in theory or in preconceived ways of looking at the world. Today, the *chengyu* is widely used to poke fun at those who cling stubbornly to the rules or adhere to dogma instead of looking at the reality in front of their eyes.

Location: Kingdom of Zheng, modern Henan province, east-central China

	Pinyin	*Pronunciation*	*Definition*
鄭	zhèng	jeng	the name of a kingdom
人	rén	ren	a man; a person or people
置	zhì	je	to install; to place; to put
履	lǚ	loo-i	a shoe; to tread on

望梅止渴 Wàng Méi Zhǐ Kě

QUENCHING THIRST BY HOPING FOR PLUMS

The author, Liu Yi Qin, who lived in the fifth century CE, used the story of the illusory plums to suggest that authorities often attempt to cheat people by giving them false hope or by offering empty gestures of goodwill. Today, the Chinese use this *chengyu* to refer to something that is false, or not practical, or not within reach. It is often heard in circumstances where someone makes baseless promises—including government officials, who too often make promises that, like the plums, ultimately fail to materialize.

Location: Kingdom of Wei, modern Hebei, Shanxi, Shaanxi, Henan, and Shandong provinces, north-central China

	Pinyin	*Pronunciation*	*Definition*
望	wàng	wung	to look toward; to hope; to expect
梅	méi	may	a plum or plum blossom
止	zhǐ	je-i	to stop; to prohibit; until
渴	kě	kuh-uh	thirsty

熟能生巧 Shú Néng Shēng Qiǎo

PRACTICE MAKES PERFECT

This story can be traced to Ouyang Xiu, who lived during the Song Dynasty (960–1279 CE). He was a renowned politician and writer, as well as a great proponent of innovation. In the story, which he dedicated to Confucius, Ouyang encourages people to succeed through hard work and practice. Diligence and study are values central to Confucianism, as is modesty. In the story, the old oil seller not only exemplifies the virtue of humility but teaches it to the proud Chen Kang Su. Nowadays, the *chengyu* is frequently invoked to encourage people to study hard, for this is the means to success.

Location: Modern Shanxi province, along the Great Wall, in north-central China

	Pinyin	Pronunciation	Definition
熟	shú	shoh	familiar; skilled; ripe; done; cooked
能	néng	nung	may; capable; able
生	shēng	shung	to be born; to give birth; to grow; life
巧	qiǎo	chee-ow	skillful; timely; as the case may be

按圖索驥　Àn Tú Suǒ Jì

LOOKING FOR A HORSE WITH THE AID OF A DIAGRAM

This story comes from a work called *Lumbering in the Forest of Art*, written by Yang Shen, a poet who lived during the Ming Dynasty (1368–1644). Yang Shen tells the story of Bo Le's son, who stubbornly used the image conjured up by a phrase in a book as a guide to identifying a horse. The story points out that when people lack practical experience, they are apt to blunder ahead mechanically, mindlessly following instructions without stopping to examine the evidence and exercise critical judgment. Today, the Chinese use this *chengyu* to warn of the foolishness of those who do not know how to modify their plans to accord with the realities of a situation or who insist on proceeding according to fixed rules.

Location: Kingdom of Qin, modern Shanxi province, north-central China

	Pinyin	Pronunciation	Definition
按	àn	ahn	according to
圖	tú	too	a diagram; a drawing; a chart
索	suǒ	su-oh	to search; to demand
驥	jì	jee	a thoroughbred horse

猴子捞月 Hóu Zi Lāo Yuè

MONKEYS DRAGGING UP THE MOON

This is a story from a Buddhist text, although most children and adults in China today know it from a popular cartoon and picture book. When people lack wisdom, like the poor monkeys, they do silly, impractical things like fishing for the moon. The monkeys have ample compassion, but they are unsuccessful in their efforts to be helpful because they forge ahead without thinking, and in the end they even lose their own lives. The story teaches us that we must be thoughtful and ascertain the truth of a situation before taking action. The *chengyu* is used these days to refer to a person who is bound to fail because his or her goal is unrealistic.

Location: Kingdom of Jiashi, modern location unknown (but somewhere near the border of India and China)

	Pinyin	*Pronunciation*	*Definition*
猴子	hóu zi	ho dzi	a monkey
捞	lāo	lao	to pull up; to drag up
月	yuè	yu-eh	the moon; a month

亡羊補牢 Wáng Yáng Bǔ Láo

MEND THE SHEEPFOLD, EVEN IF SHEEP HAVE BEEN LOST

This is another story from the *Intrigues of the Warring States*, the superb collection of historical tales complied in the first century BCE by the Confucian scholar Liu Xiang. Nowadays, the *chengyu* is used in two different, almost opposite, senses. As the story indicates, the shepherd could still save his remaining flock, but only if he made the needed repairs right away. So, on the one hand, the *chengyu* encourages people to correct their mistakes, no matter when they are discovered, so as to avoid further damage. It's much like the Western adage, "Better late than never." But the story also shows that as long as the shepherd kept his sheepfold in good repair and stayed awake at night, he was able to safeguard his entire flock. On the other hand, then, the *chengyu* warns people not to wait until an error has been made but to anticipate problems before they arise. In this sense, it's akin to the Western expression, "A stitch in time saves nine." In either case, the emphasis is on diligence. Trouble arises, the story suggests, only when we become complacent and careless.

Location: Kingdom of Chu, modern Hunan and Hubei provinces, south-central China

	Pinyin	*Pronunciation*	*Definition*
亡	wáng	wahng	to die; to perish
羊	yáng	yung	sheep
補	bǔ	boo-u	to repair; to make amends
牢	láo	lao	firm; fast

南轅北轍 Nán Yuán Běi Zhé

TRYING TO GO SOUTH BY DRIVING THE CHARIOT NORTH

Like the preceding story, this tale is also found in the *Intrigues of the Warring States*. The king of Wei is eager to gain more territory because he wishes to be revered as a supreme ruler, honored and trusted by his subjects. But, as his wise minister advises him, he cannot win respect by using his power to attack the weak. When our actions are at odds with our purpose, the story asks, how can the purpose be achieved? The tale reminds us that our direction must be clear before any progress can be made and that, in pursuing a desired result, we must use our resources thoughtfully and appropriately. Today, the Chinese use this *chengyu* to point out when someone seems to be working at cross-purposes to his or her intended goal.

Location: Kingdom of Wei (Warring States Period), modern Shanxi province, north-central China

	Pinyin	*Pronunciation*	*Definition*
南	nán	nahn	south
轅	yuán	yoo-en	the steering rod of a carriage
北	běi	bey-i	north
轍	zhé	juh	a rut; a track

齊人攫金 Qí Rén Jué Jīn

A MAN FROM THE KINGDOM OF QI SNATCHES GOLD

This story was taken from the "Explaining Conjunctions" chapter of the classic Taoist text the *Liezi*, which is attributed to Lie Yukou, a philosopher who is said to have lived in the fifth century BCE, during the period of social and political upheaval that preceded China's first unification. The story describes a person blinded by his lust for gold: excessive desire renders him incapable of seeing clearly. The events in the story are said to have taken place in the kingdom of Zheng—but when people there told the tale, they said the man was from the kingdom of Qi because they were embarrassed to be associated with such a person. In his dedication to the story, Lie Yukou urged people to keep their needs modest, which accords with the Taoist principle of simplicity and restraint (*jiǎn*). At the same time, the fact that the man who steals the gold ends up being arrested, and thus loses his freedom, suggests that we are ultimately imprisoned by our obsessions. Today, this *chengyu* and its story are used to warn people who are hungry for money or power that in the end their true motives will always be found out.

Location: Kingdom of Zheng, modern Henan province, central China, but supposedly the Kingdom of Qi (齐 Qí), modern Shandong province, east China

	Pinyin	*Pronunciation*	*Definition*
齊	qí	chee	the name of a kingdom
人	rén	ren	a man; a person or people
攫	jué	ju-eh	to seize (usually with reference to a bird or animal)
金	jīn	jin	metal; money; gold

刻舟求劍 Kè Zhōu Qíu Jiàn

MARKING THE BOAT TO SEARCH FOR YOUR SWORD IN THE RIVER

This story appears in *The Spring and Autumn Annals of Mister Lü (Lüshi Chunqiu)*, a philosophical compendium that is the work of Lü Buwei, who lived in the third century BCE and served as the chancellor of the first emperor of the Qin dynasty, under whom China was first unified. The man in the story is so limited in his thinking and so convinced that his methods are correct that, even though the world is moving right by him, he doesn't even notice. The story serves as a reminder that we must be alert to newly developing realities. The *chengyu* is often used to reproach those who seem out of touch with the world around them, which is constantly changing, and who consequently cannot deal very well with practicalities.

Location: Kingdom of Chu, modern Hunan and Hubei provinces, south-central China

	Pinyin	Pronunciation	Definition
刻	kè	kuh	to carve; to engrave; to cut; oppressive
舟	zhōu	jo	a boat
求	qíu	chee-yo	to seek; to look for; to request; to demand
劍	jiàn	jiahn	a double-edged sword

掩耳盗鈴 Yǎn Ěr Dào Líng

PLUGGING ONE'S EARS WHILE STEALING A BELL

This story is also found in Lü Buwei's *Spring and Autumn Annals of Mister Lü*. The tale pokes fun at the thief, who should have realized that the bell would make a very loud noise when he struck it: he didn't pause to think his plan through. But the story also contains a warning about self-centeredness. The thief believes that because he can't hear the bell, nobody else is able to hear it either. He foolishly assumes that his own experience is the one and only reality. The idiom is widely used in China today to make fun of those who try to deceive themselves and those around them in grandiose, short-sighted ways.

Location: Kingdom of Jin, modern Shanxi province, north-central China

	Pinyin	*Pronunciation*	*Definition*
掩	yǎn	yen	to cover up
耳	ěr	er	the ear
盗	dào	dao	to steal; a robber
鈴	líng	ling	a bell

濫竽充數　Làn Yú Chōng Shù

AN UNSKILLED MUSICIAN CONCEALED IN THE CROWD

This is another story told by the legalist philosopher Han Feizi. As a legalist and a strong supporter of the imperial throne, Han Feizi was aware that members of the royal entourage (not the least among them a king's most trusted ministers) were prone to corruption. His story advises rulers that they should pay close attention to those in their service and be on the lookout for possible freeloaders. Indeed, there are many Nan Guos among us, who aim to reap rewards without having any special abilities and without making any serious effort. The story cautions us that, in the end, when we attempt to get something for nothing, we risk being exposed as cheats. This *chengyu* is very popular in China today and is often taught to children in elementary school.

Location: Kingdom of Qi (齐 Qí), modern Shandong province, east China

	Pinyin	*Pronunciation*	*Definition*
濫	làn	la-ahn	unskilled, indiscriminate
竽	yú	yu-i	a musical instrument, somewhat like a flute
充	chōng	chong	to fill in; to act in place of; to substitute for
數	shù	shu	a number; to number; to count

塞翁失馬 Sài Wēng Shī Mǎ

OLD MAN SAI LOST HIS HORSE

This story is taken from a book called the *Huainanzi*. Its author, Liu An, who lived in the second century BCE, was a Chinese prince and an advisor to his nephew, Emperor Wu of the Han Dynasty. Legend also has it that Liu An was the inventor of tofu. The *Huainanzi* is considered by some to be one of the cornerstones of Taoist philosophy, along with the *Tao Te Ching* and the *Zhuangzi*, and the story Liu An tells is quintessentially Taoist. Sai Weng's wise father understands the Way of nature and so is able to keep his focus on the big picture, rather than being constantly thrown off balance by short-term gains and losses. His equanimity comes from knowing that both joy and sorrow are transitory—that, in the long run, happiness may result from disaster, while within good fortune disaster may lurk. Much as we say that every cloud has a silver lining, the Chinese use this *chengyu* to remind those who are beset by troubles that an unanticipated reward could be one of the fruits of their misfortune.

Location: China's northern frontier, modern Shanxi province, north China

	Pinyin	Pronunciation	Definition
塞	sài	sai	a personal name; a frontier fortress
翁	wēng	wong	an elderly person
失	shī	shi	to lose; to miss; to fail
馬	mǎ	ma-ah	a horse

愚公移山 Yú Gōng Yí Shān

YU GONG MOVED MOUNTAINS

This is another story from the Taoist classic the *Liezi*, attributed to the philosopher Lie Yukou, who is said to have lived during the fifth century BCE. The story, which appears in a chapter called "The Questions of Tang," fits a Taoist context because of the old man's patience and gentle persistence. In the same way that, over the course of many centuries, wind and water slowly wear away mountains, Yu Gong follows the gradual pace of nature, knowing that generations after him will continue his work. In modern China, however, the story has been given another reading. Determined to move mountains, Yu Gong gathers all the forces at his disposal to help him in his effort. Chairman Mao encouraged people to follow the spirit of Yu Gong by working hard to conquer and control nature—a notably un-Taoist enterprise. Viewed in this new light, the story is very popular nowadays and is taught to children as part of the elementary school curriculum.

Location: Ancient Jizhou, west of modern Shanxi province, in northern China

	Pinyin	*Pronunciation*	*Definition*
愚	yú	yoo	stupid
公	gōng	gung	a respectful term for an old person
移	yí	yee	to move; to remove
山	shān	shahn	a mountain; a hill

齿亡舌存 Chǐ Wáng Shé Cún

THE TEETH ARE GONE, BUT THE TONGUE REMAINS

This story also comes to us from the *Intrigues of the Warring States*, compiled during the first century BCE by the renowned Confucian scholar Liu Xiang. The figures in the story are Taoist, however, as is the lesson. From the story, we learn that hard or rigid things are easily worn away, whereas those that are soft and gentle endure. The story illustrates the Taoist principle of *wu wei*, which teaches that flexibility and a lack of resistance are the source of genuine strength. When we are unyielding and willful—when we attempt to force the world to conform to our wishes—we only waste our energy, which ultimately weakens us. Unlike the others in this collection, this *chengyu* is heard relatively infrequently, possibly because its message is quite abstract and philosophical. Nevertheless, it conveys a centrally important Taoist concept, one that, over the centuries, has subtly infused the Chinese worldview.

Location: None specified

	Pinyin	*Pronunciation*	*Definition*
齿	chǐ	chuh	a tooth
亡	wáng	wahng	to die; to perish
舌	shé	shuh	the tongue
存	cún	tswun	to exist; to survive

Acknowledgments

We are immensely grateful to Ji Ruoxiao for lending her phenomenal artistic talents to this project and to our friends and family for their unflagging support. We also wish to thank the team at Eastern Washington University Press—especially Ivar Nelson, for his encouragement, and Pamela MacFarland Holway, for her extraordinary editing—and designer Rich Hendel, for giving us a magnificent book.

SARAH CONOVER's interests lie with world traditions of wisdom and spirituality. She holds a BA in religious studies from the University of Colorado, a degree in education from Gonzaga University, and an MFA in poetry from Eastern Washington University. *Harmony* is her fourth book in the This Little Light of Mine series, of which she is the founder and general editor. The inaugural volume, *Kindness*, a collection of Buddhist tales, was recommended by *Booklist* as one of the five best spiritual books for children of 2001, while the second, *Ayat Jamilah: Beautiful Signs*, was cited by *Newsweek* as one of the best multicultural books of 2004 and was also the winner of the 2004 Aesop Prize, presented by the American Folklore Society. In addition, Conover was a contributing coeditor of the third volume in the series, *At Work in Life's Garden: Writers on the Spiritual Adventure of Parenting*, a collection of literary essays. She is also the coauthor of *Daughters of the Desert: Remarkable Women from the Christian, Jewish, and Muslim Traditions* (SkylightPaths Press, 2003). Her poetry has appeared in *Rock and Sling*, the *Santa Clara Review*, and *Pontoon 10*, as well as in the anthology *Family Pictures*.

Conover lives in Spokane, Washington, where she teaches English and radio production. Through her own writing, as well as through international collaborations with other educators, she strives to bring multicultural perspectives to youth, in and out of the classroom. She has participated in many cross-cultural projects, from the Middle East to Brazil. Prior to her work as a writer and public educator, she was a senior producer for Internews, an international NGO committed to fostering open media around the world. In that capacity, she was the American producer for the United Nations television series *Agenda for a Small Planet*, which aired in thirty-three countries. She also produced the National Academy of Science's *The Medical Implications of Nuclear War*, in addition to many programs for public television.

CHEN HUI 陳慧 was born in 1966, at the very start of the Cultural Revolution, in Changsha, the capital of Hunan province. That same year her father was removed by the government from his position as an engineer and taken to the countryside to work as a farm laborer for ten years. He was determined to see his daughter learn English, however, and asked a friend of his to begin teaching her. Hui eventually majored in English literature and education at Hunan Normal University, following which she served as the director of the International Office at the Hunan University of Economics, as well as at the Central South University of Forestry and Technology, both in Chansha. She then moved to the United States, earning an MA in education from Harding University, in Searcy, Arkansas. Her professional career has led her to teach English in China, to place English teachers in Chinese schools, and to teach Chinese in English-speaking schools, most recently at St. George's School, in Spokane, Washington, and much of her life's work has thus been devoted to building bridges between China and the United States. Having also made an informal study of ancient Chinese literature for many years, she is always delighted to have the opportunity to share traditional Chinese culture with Western friends. *Harmony* is her first book.

JI RUOXIAO 季若霄 has been a professor of art at Sichuan Normal University, in Chengdu, for twenty years. She graduated in fine arts from Southwestern Normal University, in Chongqing, and completed advanced studies at the Central Institute of Fine

Arts in Beijing, generally acknowledged as the China's preeminent fine arts academy. She lives in Seattle and returns each year to Sichuan to teach.

At the First National Art Exhibition of Chinese Landscape Painting, Ruoxiao was honored with the Selected Work Award, and she received the Maple Leaf Award at the International Oriental Sumi Art Exhibition. Her paintings are in the collection of the Chinese Art Museum, in Beijing, and in 1995 she was one of two Chinese artists whose work was chosen for the art exhibition at the Fourth United Nations World Conference of Women. She is the author of three books on the theory and technique of Chinese brush painting and has lectured at the University of California at Berkeley, the San Francisco Art Institute, and Washington State University.

The This Little Light of Mine series seeks to broaden our knowledge of and perspective on world traditions of wisdom and spirituality. By gathering and adapting material from primary texts, many of them quite ancient, we aim to open windows onto wisdom as it was, and continues to be, conceived and lived in cultures around the globe. The books in the series are intended to engage children, young adults, educators, and parents alike, and we hope they will foster many spirited and rewarding discussions.

Given the flood of information in which we are daily inundated, it is striking how seldom one hears the word *wisdom*. T. S. Eliot once asked, "Where is the knowledge that is lost in information? Where is the wisdom that is lost in knowledge?" Rarely do we ponder such questions. And yet, from time immemorial, people everywhere have asked, *What's truly important?* The question has been asked in a myriad of ways, and the world's wisdom traditions represent a myriad of replies. These traditions tell us what is most valued in a particular culture, and why. They encompass a culture's collective, and enduring, thinking on deep and difficult matters.

Much as we might prefer to separate politics and religion, both deal in the currency of values. How can we engage another culture unless we have some familiarity with the philosophical concepts, ethical principles, and spiritual beliefs that animate and guide it? Whether we teach social studies or simply discuss the day's news with family around the dinner table, we cannot fully understand the motivations—so often grounded in faith—that drive world events unless we know something of the moral and metaphysical underpinnings of societies other than our own. In *The Illustrated World's Religions,*

Huston Smith rightly argues that the times require us listen to other cultures — that in our ever shrinking, ever more interconnected world, the essential understanding that comes from listening is the only place that peace can find a home.

Young or old, we are all citizens of the world now. We are, additionally, all students of life, from birth onward. Not only do small children ask big questions just about as soon as they can string a sentence together — *Why are we here? What's it all about?* — but young adults also thirst for discussion of philosophical and spiritual issues. How should we live? What makes someone a good person — and does virtue still have value? What gives life meaning? Why is there suffering in the world? As our children face their tomorrows, they are anxious to know how others have grappled with life's dilemmas and sorrows and absurdities.

We need courage to look beyond our own understandings of life, courage to consult and to profit from the wisdom traditions of humankind. It is our hope that the volumes in the This Little Light of Mine series will play some small role in furthering cross-cultural understanding and in building homes and schools in which peace can flourish.

Kindness: A Treasury of Buddhist Wisdom for Children and Parents (2001). Collected and adapted by Sarah Conover. With illustrations by Valerie Wahl.

Ayat Jamilah: Beautiful Signs: A Treasury of Islamic Wisdom for Children and Parents (2004). Collected and adapted by Sarah Conover and Freda Crane. With illustrations by Valerie Wahl.

At Work in Life's Garden: Writers on the Spiritual Adventure of Parenting (2005). Edited by Sarah Conover and Tracy Springberry.

Harmony: A Treasury of Chinese Wisdom for Children and Parents (2008). Collected and adapted by Sarah Conover and Chen Hui. With illustrations by Ji Ruoxiao.